Salvation

Lucia Nevai

TinHouseBooks

Copyright © 2008 Lucia Nevai

Additional copyright permissions appear on page 216.

Published by Tin House Books, Portland, Oregon, and New York, New York
Distributed to the trade by Publishers Group West,
1700 Fourth St., Berkeley, CA 94710,
www.pgw.com

Library of Congress Cataloging-in-Publication Data

Nevai, Lucia, 1945-
Salvation / Lucia Nevai.
p. cm.
ISBN 978-0-9794198-3-6
1. Young women--Fiction. 2. Native Americans--Fiction. 3. Poor families--Fiction.
4. Domestic fiction. I. Title.
PS3564.E848S25 2008
813'.54--dc22   2008004003

First U.S. edition 2008

ISBN 10: 0-9794198-3-2

Interior design by Laura Shaw Design, Inc.

www.tinhouse.com

Printed in Canada

For my father,
Darwin Thomas Lynner

Prologue

With abject, slavish desire, with off-hand, sloppy curiosity, with gratitude, with sedation, I was accidentally engendered. Never say the word *rid* around me. My mother tried to get rid of me. My face to this day is deformed, my forehead bumpy, puffy, and white as mold. Her attempt was halfhearted; her method unknown. Where do I feel it? In the lungs. It comes back in winter when I wheeze. It comes back when I feel cowardly. There's pressure, slight at first, and frontal, then heavier and from all sides, as if I'm in a crushing machine that will reduce my mass to a minus number. Through it all, I'm hyperventilating, sucking oxygen as hard as I can, turning and twisting in my close, red space, inhaling all the *O*s I can find. Oxygen, that cool, sweet, slender thread of life I love. *Ooooooooooooooooo.*

She failed. She let me live. With my big head softened up like that, I tried to go easy on her when I was born. Now, I failed. She pushed me out to the tune of a thousand and one blue curses. Given a choice, I would have stayed inside. She was glad I was out of her life and on my own. She put on lipstick and left the hospital.

It was an unpleasant interval. Where was her smell? I missed the sound of her voice echoing down through her innards to me. I'd grown used to its tone, its twang. Sometimes she sang. I missed our drugs, whatever they were. The rubber nipple held begrudgingly by the nurse delivered squeaky-clean nutrition. I refused it at first, looking for whatever it was I was used to. The nurse felt miffed and cut me off. Lacking our tranquilizers, disgusted by formula, I could have used a cigarette. No luck there either. People to the right and left of me were bawling. I gave it a try. Out came half a coo. I didn't have the lungs for bellowing, thanks to you-know-who. I gave up wanting anything. That seemed to work. My first successful approach to life! I would remember it always.

Sunlight was entrancing. Neither too simple nor too complex. It was substanceless, yet it filled up the four pink nursery walls, entering the room in shafts, structures it accepted from the windows interspersed along the wall. Motes and flecks suspended in the air were illuminated by it as if they were valuable. There seemed to be more than enough of it outside the window. Sunlight: warm, silky, intelligent, unlimited, impartial, kind, unfathomable. I waved my fist in it, stirring it up, introducing a new smell that wrinkled my nose, the smell of bleach. All around me, people were wailing. I blew one bubble. I felt inadequate, envying their freedom, wondering what it would be like to throw back your head and let loose, test-driving a pair of healthy, new, red-blooded lungs.

—

Lying in the nursery, busy with its light, sniffing the air for any hint of lipstick, my ears ringing with the racket around me, a part of me loses heart. An institution is colder and emptier than a person, even if that person is sick of you.

I assume things. X is out there. I want her in here. I may not get what I want. I might get Y, the nurse I don't want. The greatest question underlying all of this is time, the time between wanting and getting, between X and Y. I wait. Waiting means flowing sideways in time so it carries you along without shearing off something you might need later. It works: I feel loved by the light. The womb was dark. I could never tell if I was dreaming my dream in there or hers.

—

Outside of the hospital entrance, parked at the curb, is a blue car. My mother in her red dress must have descended to the lobby in the elevator in a state of intolerable withdrawal. She must have settled her beautiful bottom down into the soft front seat of the roadster at the curb. She's counting the minutes. She must have turned to the man at the wheel with something of a promise, something of a plea. She sends the two children in the backseat up the hospital steps for me.

My brother is seven, my sister five. He's comfortable in his skin, she's ashamed of hers. Douglas Cavanaugh, Jr., that's his given name. They call him Little Duck. He has that kind of beauty that's startling in a man. I don't mean the baby-face cuteness. I mean beauty, the Jesus kind, that makes people want to follow you and devour you.

My sister Jima wears a yellow dress. Buttons are missing. Her shoulders twist in place as she tries not to take up space. Her sweetness and allure are sidelong. Her long, brown, dusty ponytail is half out of the clasp. Her teeth are crooked, turning a corner suddenly in the middle of her smile, like Big Duck's before the dentures. Her pale gray eyes can see for miles. Her eyebrows are dusty; her elbows and forearms are dusty. Her knees, her feet. Everything about her is dusty. Where we live, the wind blows grit from the played-out gravel mine into our pores. The air sifts fine black silt from the cornfields into our hair. Silent, dusty, and barefooted, they stand there looking very much like children who don't belong in public. The dirt and their bare feet erase how good-looking they are. This is the first public building they've seen. It's quiet for its size and solidity. The unnatural hush in the halls seems to help along the doctors and nurses with the importance of their jobs. Little Duck and Jima are used to a floor that's soft and pliant, built of hand-sawn planks of pine. This floor's hard and cold, gleaming granite, rank with disinfectant. Little Duck lopes across it. Jima moves forward uncertainly, step by step, looking down at her feet so she doesn't make a mistake.

They pass a row of chairs, somber, upholstered things meant for visitors. A man is sitting in one, reading a magazine, smoking, flicking ashes into a large, strong, freestanding steel ashtray. There's the whooshing sound of a great weight falling evenly through the air, accompanied by a humming that gets louder and louder. The humming terminates abruptly in a hydraulic sigh. A pair of steel doors glides apart, disappearing into the lobby wall. Large, clean, well-dressed people are standing there, trapped inside a steel box recessed in the wall, though they don't seem upset. In fact, they seem bored. My brother and sister jump out of their path as they walk into the lobby.

"Goin' up?" The black man in the green suit who's driving this thing is talking to Little Duck. The man sits on a half stool that unfolds from the elevator wall. His right hand holds half a steering wheel, his left hand holds a knob that opens and shuts the big steel doors with folding Xs. His white hair is tightly curled like pubic hair. Little Duck and Jima stare at the pink skin of the man's gums and palms, wondering if the black color will eventually wear off the rest of him too. The man begins to laugh merrily, a skittering laugh full of "K" sounds as air is scraped against the roof of his mouth. His shoulders jump up and down with joy. "James is you fust niggah!" he says. "Y'all ain't nevah seena niggah befo'. Doan be 'fray. Step in-sigh." They slip inside the elevator car quick, afraid of the doors. "What flo?" he says. They don't know. "Who y'all heah fo' to see?"

"A baby," Little Duck says.

"Thas three." As James slides the knob, the Xs flatten into horizontals, closing the doors with the heavy, rolling sound of oiled steel. A whorling feeling inside their stomachs tells my brother and sister they're moving, but they can't tell if they're going up or down. They cling to the wall to steady themselves. When James opens the doors at the pink walls of Pediatrics, Little Duck and Jima won't get off. They're afraid of falling through the dark, inchwide gap of nothingness between the elevator car and the granite floor.

"Doan look down," James says. "Look straight and fly o'er." They do. The floor they land on doesn't move. They watch gratefully as James pulls the steel doors shut again, locking himself in. They find their way to the newborns, surprising the nurse. She's snickering now, pointing out ugly me to Dr. Prescott as he makes his rounds with his cold metal stethoscope, checking our hearts. I'm lying there in my hospital bassinet, wrapped in my white flannel blanket, wearing my white cotton infant gown, not knowing what to expect, when I smell our dirt. Hoo-ray! Little Duck and Jima are standing in the doorway. They watch as the nurse flirtatiously removes the doctor's authoritative, horn-rimmed eyeglasses and places them on my soft, newborn, disfigured face. I look about forty. The nurse laughs hard. A mean laugh that excludes everyone but herself and Dr. Prescott.

The doctor is taken aback. He is a literal man and can't see all that well without his glasses. The nurse is rough as she picks me up with the doctor's huge horn-rims balancing precariously on my small, soft bump of a nose. She thinks I'm inanimate—I can tell by the jerky shove of her thumbs on my ribs. I'd like to shove her back some day. She uses me as a puppet to poke a little innocent fun at the doctor. "Give the bitch more gas—I want peace and quiet around here," she says, imitating his voice exactly. That sends him into hysterics, a frightening sound, the sound of a controlled person finally letting loose. She laughs with him, following the up-and-down of his voice in an intimate, explicit way that tries to draw the attention back to her.

Bravery makes Jima defiant. When she's angry, her pale gray eyes grow dark and speckled. Her sidelong approach is cast aside for a direct one, born of conviction. She walks straight up to the nurse. Little Duck is right behind her. "What are you two doing here?" the nurse says, reversing the blame. She gives Dr. Prescott his glasses back. "You're to wait at the nurse's station," she says. But my brother and sister don't move. He's beautiful and calm with his deep-eyed stare. She's mad and insistent. Nobody makes fun of their little sister. Jima holds out her arms to take me. The nurse hands me over. In the lightness of the touch of Jima's hands, the careful, tender placement of the palms, in the protective crook of the elbow, in the lub-dub whisper of the heart through her yellow dress, I feel important. I feel love. I am a new little me that my sister wants. *Whatever I have is yours*, her heart says to me through her dress. The nurse presents the clipboard to my brother. He signs me out with an *X*. Off we go. Jima steadies me against the topsy-turvy flying motion of the elevator. She carries me through the hush of the lobby. She braces me against the smell of lipstick in the front seat of the blue car. My dangerous mother is near. I'm thrilled, though I react by holding my breath. I will have to get used to the tinny, distant sound of her voice in the air outside of the womb. Big Duck is at the wheel in his white hat. The sight of me rankles him. It comes across as a single, sludgy green wave of hate issued from his jaw. His lips curl with pleasure at the sight of my disfiguration. It serves me right. He smells like whisky and cigarettes. I need one, but I don't know how to ask.

He drives away, making my brain spin, my insides queasy. Jima steadies me against the flying motion of the road. There are careening twists and turns that throw our bodies left and right. There are dips and bumps that send our stomachs into flips. There is the taste and smell and weight of dust, Iowa dust, dust rising in funnels that jet forth from our tires where the tread bites into the dirt, rising, rising up into the air, sifting down, down through the top of the open window, settling ever so gently and companionably on our skins. The road home. It's a much wilder ride than when I was inside.

|

There was a boy on the ceiling. He was hairless, but not in a way that would upset anyone. His mood was both passive and recalcitrant—people who thought his silence meant they could talk him into things had better think again. He was always quiet, never complaining, always at peace, never at odds, always resigned, never ambitious, always sad, never happy. *I like you*, I thought. No reaction from him. During the day, whenever I looked up, he was there. At night, he came down from the rafters to sleep, light as a feather, between Jima and me. He settled his shoulders against mine. Jima watched me closely to see if I could feel it. He stayed there until she fell asleep, then he floated back up to the ceiling.

—

My mother was the one in red. Her eyes were moist, dark, half-closed, her lashes long, her lovely arching brows wonderful to look at. Her hair was a dark fountain of waves. She had those high Sioux cheekbones, that red skin. Her eyes were the ideal distance apart, her nose the ideal length. Her lips were shaped like secret knowledge. Her figure was more obvious.

Big, dreamy, creamy breasts. Big promising hips. In between, a small waist. Below, slender curving calves and narrow pretty ankles. The neckline of her red dress was cut low. Her name was Letitia. Everyone called her Tit. She took her time at things. She knew why she did what she did. Allure clung to her and followed her. It gave her an authority that, in turn, made her feel unloved and alone.

Jima's mother was the one in blue. They called us sisters so often, we forgot we weren't. Her mother's name was Flaherty. They called her Flat. Flat sat at the piano in a slack, blue, threadbare chemise, chewing her fingernails, disapproving of Tit. Her eyes were colorless and excessively bright. Her large Irish chin was flat with extra obedience to God. Her forehead and cheeks were flat too, as if the bones in her face were not permitted to mature. Flat was married to Big Duck, but he was in love with Tit. The three of them met on the revival circuit—they were all saved by the same great itinerant healer. Salvation didn't last. Even we three ignorant kids could see that.

—

We lived in the sturdy, two-room wooden shack with the steep roof situated between the railroad tracks and the gravel pit. Our three preacher-parents found the shack just in time for Little Duck to be born. They were kicked out of the revival, left behind in a thunderstorm. They drove blindly north and west in Big Duck's dark blue roadster out of Missouri into Iowa—with Tit in labor, no less. The pit boss had abandoned the shack the year before when the mine was played out. Our parents were lucky they found it, lucky it was empty, lucky there was a pump at the sink that pumped cool, delicious water, lucky there was a woodstove. The pit boss even left a little wood, praise the Lord. Our life as squatters began.

Tit named Little Duck *Douglas Cavanaugh, Jr.*, after Big Duck, briefly tricking Big Duck into the pride of paternity. Little Duck had Tit's cheekbones, her red skin. But he soon developed his real father's unmistakable, magnetic, deep-eyed stare. Without ever meeting his father, the world-famous Welsh evangelist and healer Clinton S. Farnsworth, Little Duck began to comb his hair in a careful pompadour exactly the same way. In the glove compartment, we found photos. The two Ducks despised each other.

Jima came next. She *was* Big Duck's, but that didn't balance things out for him. She was a girl, and not just any girl, an insecure, skinny little girl with flat cheeks and a flat forehead, hungry to please, just like Flat. Big Duck was uninterested.

There was an interval of confusion. Something terrible happened.

—

My mother named me *Crane*, after her unfortunate Sioux mother, both of us referring to the gray wading bird. My father was a pharmacist. I looked like him, middle-aged. Only our brains were beautiful. Shimmering weights and dark measures balanced each other all around me in hidden, numberless laws. The raw wood of our steep roof instructed me, exposing the load-bearing mechanics of loft and height. Light streaks zigzagged across the wooden rafters, compressing on the zig, stretching on the zag, with a volume that was fixed. I watched the sky breathe in and out, wasting nothing.

Jima heard the mood of me, the high-speed, high-frequency hum. My aptitude alarmed her. It was foreign and modern, as advanced as the elevator. With primitive cunning, she hid it from our parents, inserting herself between them and me. She felt compelled to keep me alive. She guessed at my needs. I woke up parched, hallucinating. She pumped cold water into the tin cup. It tasted of iron. I drank it down. She refilled it twice and made me drink. My brain felt moister. Her turn. We snuck over to the liquor bottle. She unscrewed the cap. Her pale gray eyes closed beatifically as the whisky hit her tongue and rolled back through her mouth to her throat. All the fortitude and consolation she needed to love and protect me the rest of the day she got from Big Duck's whisky while he slept, in sips so little he couldn't tell, or if he could, he thought it was Tit, which it also was.

She showed me where we were supposed to shit. We took turns. It worked. I reached the age of three.

———

We stood at the fence, the three of us, watching the farmer farm. The engine of his tractor echoed on the horizon, saddle-stitching a layer of sound to the soft morning sky. Little Duck understood what he saw, effortlessly construing things about machines that he would use to build a beautiful life. In his tight, ripped Levi's and pompadour, with his deep stare, Little Duck was his own man. Jima in her yellow dress spotted the animals and birds. "Look, Crane," she said, and pointed at something remarkable. Maybe it was a hawk circling below the clouds of the western horizon. I pretended to be excited. "What is it?" she would ask. I failed to answer. My eyesight was terrible. She would try again. "Crane," she said, "can you see that?" Maybe it was a stag the color of dusk standing stock-still at the edge of the woods, listening. I nodded my head yes, lunging up and down at the knees to show excitement. "No, you can't," she said, embarrassing me.

My eyes were bad, but I had the best nose. Standing at the fence in the morning with Little Duck and Jima, my nostrils would wrinkle. I would turn toward the door. I could smell my mother swinging her legs over the edge of the cot, reaching down for the red robe she kept on the floor.

"Come here, you little shits," Tit called to Jima and me. "You too, big shit," she said, calling to Little Duck. We three slunk back into the shack and lined up at her side. She dropped white pills down our throats. "Don't you little bastards go sayin' nobody never gave you no A for longevity, no B6 for nerves, no C for strong gums like Tit just done for you now," she said, one challenging eye on Flat. "You got yer D for good teeth, yer E for eyes and skin."

We swallowed and swallowed. When the swallowing was done, Flat called us to prayer to undo Tit's blasphemy. Flat's voice scraped against her throat like a hiss. "Life everlasting will be yours if you will trust in God," she said. "If it is God's will that you be free of sickness, then you will be free of sickness. If it's God's will that you be free of disease, then you will be free of disease." To appease her, we all burped, as if the vitamins didn't agree with us. That was it—our mothering was done. Long life. Life everlasting. Forced on us in quick succession, the things our mothers stood for were mutually exclusive. Each of them truly believed the other was corrupting us, ruining our futures while stealing our loyalty. We understood that the impulse behind these competing tyrannies was love—all the love we were going to get. Little Duck took his and went back outside. Jima and me covered for him. We stayed. Tit dropped her robe and stood there naked for a while. Then she put on her garter belt. Slowly, carefully, because she hated runs, she pulled on her fishnet stockings. She slipped the red dress over her head. She clasped the gold cross and chain around her neck, which in her case had the opposite of the chaste effect, drawing your attention straight down into her glorious cleavage. She looked in the mirror to brush her wavy brown hair. She powdered her beautiful high cheekbones. Her cleavage. Her neck. She glistened. She drew red lipstick over her lips. She packed her order pad into her Vita-Life home demonstration kit. My mother was an official representative for Vita-Life's complete line of vitamins, herbal remedies, and health supplements. She squirted on perfume and walked out the door without ever washing her face. She took her smell with her, causing a part of me to feel off balance until she returned.

"Let us sing," Flat said to Jima and me. She made it sound like hard work. We watched her drop her hands down onto the piano keys with excess precision. On the revival circuit, Flat could sight-read anything in *Praises in Song*, even the hard hymns set in the key of C-flat major, which had seven flats, or the key of C-sharp major, which had seven sharps. Now, to punish us, she only played mean-spirited hymns. "This may be your last invitation," she sang at us, pointing the words into our faces in a cold, harsh stream. We winced and joined in on the chorus:

O come, come, come, come,
Come while the spirit is calling,

O come to the Savior today,
This may be your last invitation,
Sinner, come and no longer delay.

"Let us pray," Flat said. We bowed our heads, looking at each other out of the corners of our eyes, waiting. When Flat prayed silently, she was asking God to make certain people do certain things. Here it came, the sound of Big Duck waking up, walking sleepily across the floor. "Praise the Lord," Flat said, taking the credit.

Big Duck leaned in the doorway in his skivvies, stretching and yawning, scratching his bites, cursing lightly at his fleas. We all had fleas. Flat gazed at Big Duck as if he were God. Duck, in turn, gazed out the window at the road where Tit had walked into town in her fishnet stockings and high heels.

Big Duck took an hour at the sink, washing his face ever so thoroughly, ever so lovingly, washing his neck, his shoulders, his armpits. Washing his lovely privates, front and back. His feet. He was touchy about his time at the sink—everyone stayed out of his way until he was through. He shaved. He combed his hair. He donned his white dress shirt, his blue silk trousers. He buckled the belt. He flipped the pointed end of his red tie around his right shoulder, then his left, like a lariat, in order to get the knot just right. The blue silk jacket—that went on next. He was pleased with himself. He had turned into Reverend Douglas Cavanaugh—he introduced himself as "Reverend," though he wasn't a real one.

He had glittering black eyes, gleaming black hair, very white, straight false teeth. He wasn't quite handsome, but he possessed an aura of quiet power that made a person taking orders from him feel important. When he strode into the room, his jaw took charge. It worked you in silence. Before you knew it, you were looking to it for approval and your next move. In the mirror, he preached to himself for good luck. "If ye have faith as a grain of mustard seed, nothing shall be impossible unto you." He put on his hat—white straw with a navy band. God help you if you ever, ever touched, let alone crushed, that hat. He drove into town. The pool hall was open.

—

Afternoons, we were on our own. We looked idle, but we weren't. We were intensely occupied every waking moment, busy obeying our instincts, following our gut feelings, drifting toward heat, light, food, water, and love—as compulsively as paramecia. People who saw us may not have understood why we were standing somewhere, doing something, anymore than we did, but we knew we needed it, so we found it, whatever, wherever it was. If hard fact told us we were hungry, we chewed on a belt. We sucked on the cotton hems of our clothes. We ate silt. We drank elements out of the air. We became inert. We sat beneath the tree in the afternoon, hallucinating. Hallucination was the free drug of the unfed. We sat there, watching night fall, waiting to be thrilled and organized by the 9:49.

The Burlington line ran southbound at night from Chicago to Omaha and Kansas City, carrying coal, grain, wood, and paper west. We could feel it coming for twenty miles. It began with a thrumming in the ground that tickled and teased our feet and our bones. We three gravitated to the tracks and stood in a dusty cluster by the white wooden X of the railroad crossing sign, waiting with quiet, hushed, personal excited desire as if for food or sex. With a great, chilling, all-enveloping two-tone chord, sixty cars of charging, rolling tonnage came pouring out of the east toward us. The engineer saw us and pulled the whistle. We waved. The linked cars went strobing past us, rhythmically, interminably blotting out everything on the other side of the tracks except for subliminal vertical flashes of night between cars that implied the world was still there. It took so long, we forgot everything but the train, car after rolling car of great, blank weight. Then it was gone, disappearing with a lonely after-rumble through a slit at the bend of the universe. We felt improved. We felt our brains had been neatly aligned, our souls purified by sound. Truth be told, the train did more to cleanse and purify us than Jesus Christ our Lord and Personal Savior, beginning with coming every night right on time.

—

Sunday mornings when the pool hall was closed, Big Duck would lean against the wall on the back two legs of the chair, his tie loosened, his hat pushed back on his head, listening to the radio preacher preach. The steady blue stream of smoke from his Lucky would twist like a ribbon as it rose from his hand into the air, avoiding his hat. Flat sat sweetly on the piano stool in her blue dress, looking at Duck as if he were God. He called to us three. Little Duck defiantly disobeyed. He walked outside and stood at the fence. Jima and me ran to Big Duck's knee. He wanted to demonstrate for us how ineffective the radio preacher was. Tit stayed in the back room, sitting on the edge of the cot, nodding out, eyes half-closed, legs falling open, immodestly separating the front panels of her red robe. Her feet were twitching.

"On my worst day, I was better than him," Big Duck would say. "Where's the call? If you're going to take away people's hope, you've got to replace it with something. You've got to get them hungry for God deep down inside. You've got to begin with a psalm of praise." He turned off the radio with a loud click to prove it. He used to preach to hundreds. Now it was just us.

"O sing unto the Lord a new song: sing unto the Lord, all the earth," he chanted in his beautiful, persuasive baritone.

He *was* better. "Sing unto the Lord, bless his name; shew forth his salvation from day to day." His powerful, swaying, singsong voice put the emphasis on a word when you least expected it. "Declare his glory among the heathen, his wonders among all people. For the Lord *is* great and greatly to be praised: he *is* to be feared above all gods." We were suddenly with him, we completely agreed, yes, yes, the Lord *was* great and greatly to be *praised*.

He told us stories from the Bible, leaning forward, making intense eye contact with each of us in turn, then craning his neck to see into the back room where Tit was nodding out at the edge of the cot. Was she looking his way, was she listening? He knew how to carry us along on his voice through each sequential stage of the story. And even though we often knew how the story would end, Big Duck surprised us, twisting things neatly around to reveal the moral—always one of the teachings of Jesus. Our favorite—we said it out loud along with him every time—was the Golden Rule: "All things whatsoever ye would that men should do to you, do ye even so to them."

"Amen," he said. He signaled Flat. Flat dropped her hands down into the keys. The chords she played were plodding, the refrain stuffy. The words formed unmelodious mouthfuls. *Pavillioned in splendor. Girded with praise.* Big Duck's face clouded over. It was Tit he wanted to hear sing, not Flat. Tit with her crystal-clear high notes, her husky low notes, and all the notes in between, drenched in rhythm like the rhythm of the black gospel choirs. Tit singing, "He Lifted Me." *From sinking sand He lifted me, With tender hand He lifted me, From shades of night to plains of light, O praise his name, He lifted me.*

Tit singing, "What Would I Do Without Jesus." *Oh, what would I do without Jeee-sus, When the days with their shadows grow dim; When the doubt billows roll, sweeping over my soul, then what would I do without Him?* I had to agree. The woman could sing. I'd heard her in the womb. She only sang for herself these days. She only sang when she knew she was alone.

Big Duck craned his neck to see into the back room. Tit was in a world of her own. Anxiety filled his dark eyes. She was slipping right through his fingers. All this time he had been trying to impress *her*—not us; save *her*—not us.

———

A surly mood would come over Big Duck Sunday afternoons. He would take it out on me. My disfiguration entitled him to humiliate me in front of our mothers. I became his dupe. It made me feel useful, as if I were doing my part to keep him home. He would call me to his side. I'd come running. I stood at his knee. He'd ask me if I wanted a treat. I'd nod happily. I gobbled up whatever he gave, then, as Tit and Flat laughed, I ran outside to spit it out. The drink he told me was root beer was bitter coffee. The vanilla shake, foaming with bubbles, was sour milk. The special apple was a raw red potato. Jima watched, waiting for them to stop, knowing it helped us both for them to think I was a fool. Afterward, Jima and me sat together under the tree, waiting for dark. When the people in charge of you didn't learn from their mistakes, you had to, but without ever letting them know.

———

Friday nights, we would get ready for the argument. Little Duck would move farther away down the fence, his back to the shack. The boy on the ceiling would disappear. Tit would be lying on the cot, her head propped up on her arm, thumbing through the new Vita-Life catalog. She'd been to town to her post office box and cashed her check. Now she was ready. Flat sat at the piano, praying. Jima and me cringed in the corner of the shack. We were all waiting for Big Duck.

I smelled road dust. I sniffed and squinted, twisting toward the railroad tracks. There was a special pattern of fanned-out dirt that Big Duck made with his tires as he took the curves, hurtling back home in the blue roadster to fight with Tit. We all listened to the sound of Big Duck's tires bumping over the tracks. "Praise the Lord," Flat said at the piano, taking the credit for his return.

Big Duck walked in the door, his tie loosened, his hat pushed back on his head, his jaw surly. He reached under the sink for his whisky bottle. There was one swig left. He drank that. He sat down. "Letitia," he said in his booming baritone voice, hammering the bottom of the empty bottle against the wood of the tabletop. "You been sneaking shots again." Jima and me both held our breath. One of these days, if they worked together, they would figure out who else snuck shots.

From the cot, Tit sent a purple wave of contempt Big Duck's way. She turned the page of the Vita-Life catalog with a loud snap. *Some people around here work for a living*, the page said. He rattled the bottle against the table. "I said." His tone was nasty. He was already drunk. Why, we wondered, did he need to drink more? "Somebody's been sneaking shots. Letitia."

We heard a rustle. She was there in the doorway, wrapped in a great, soft, palpable lack of interest in Big Duck. Part of that was an act, or why would she arrange to be home early every payday to conduct the argument? "*Sneak*," she said. "I don't sneak nothin'. I take. Take what I want."

The sight of her made Big Duck lose his concentration. He tried to hide it, playing at maintaining that certain drunken gruffness that came so easily to him long ago when Tit was under his thumb. He cocked his head at her and tapped the empty bottle once. "Replenish." He tried for a military, no-compromise tone.

An amused look occupied Tit's face without her features ever shifting. "Big word," she said. "Wish I'd a thought a it. All those nights. I sat here. While you hustled pool. Waitin' for you to bring home a crust a bread. Never did see no bread."

"Jesus said take no thought for your life," Flat piped up, siding with Big Duck. "What ye shall eat, or what ye shall drink; nor yet for your body, what ye shall put on. Is not the life more than meat, and the body more than raiment?" Flat's voice scraped the air like an insect. They ignored her.

"Neither a you never did nothin' ta put food on the table," Tit said. "With three little shits ta feed."

Three little shits. There should have been four.

"They're your little shits, not mine," Big Duck said.

"What about that sweet little thing all skin and bones over there in the corner," Tit said. Jima cringed, twisting her face to the wall. "She cried all night. Neither a you never did get up to give her no bottle. *I* got up. And she ain't even mine, talkin' 'bout yours and mine. I give her water with whisky in it I bought and paid for by myself. Only nourishment she got. As God is my witness," Tit said.

"Take a looka that one," Big Duck said, pointing his long, straight arm out the window at Little Duck. Little Duck stood at the fence with his back to all this. "Ya gave him my name. Ya said he was mine. And then he turns out to have the same hair as Clinton S. Farnsworth. I never liked that hair on Farnsworth. And I like it worse on any kid in my house."

Tit took her time answering Big Duck. She looked in the mirror at her own hair. Her tone was relaxed. "What did you think I was doing with Clinton all those nights? Crocheting doilies? Poor old man had *trouble sleeping*," Tit said. Big Duck's face retreated. "He come to me for *company in the Lord*," Tit said. Big Duck's bravado leaked out of his features. She was quoting him. And none of his quotes were his own. He'd run away from home and joined the revival at the age of nine to escape his violent, pigheaded father, a destitute tenant farmer from the Ozark Mountains. Gesture for gesture, phrase for phrase, at the microphone and with the ladies, Big Duck copied the man who saved him, Clinton S. Farnsworth.

"Clinton S. Farnsworth would never marry no whore," Big Duck said.

"There is no whore in the eyes a God," Tit said. "*He maketh his sun to rise on the evil and on the good*, I was told. *He sendeth rain on the just and on the unjust*, the way I heard it." Duck was tongue-tied. Tit laughed her long, wise, patient laugh, a laugh that showed him—showed all of us if we cared to see it—how most of the time we bored her. She was her own best company. "What did you two think I was discussing with Clinton all night that night in the moonlight in Hickman, Missouri, when neither of us never come to bed until four in the morning?" Tit said, her tone still languorous and patient. She let our group silence collect in a pool. We could just see poor oversexed Farnsworth ruining his reputation for the love of Tit. "I wouldn't be caught dead," Tit said, "going back to Wales as a preacher's wife."

"You told me you never went with him because you loved me," Big Duck said. He was holding his hat by the brim in front of him with both hands, leaning forward submissively on the chair, his dark eyes pleading.

"I did love you," Tit said. This was the only part of the argument Big Duck liked.

"That's a helluva God damn way to prove it," he said. "By turning out to be a God damn two-timer."

"Thou shalt not take the name of the Lord thy God in vain," Flat said, looking straight at Tit. She was afraid to reprimand her husband directly or he might leave again for two years. He might go back to his first wife and children.

"*Two-timer*," Tit repeated, slowly raising her beautiful eyebrows as if she were intrigued, savoring the concept, emphasizing the relevancy of its meaning to certain others present in the room, nodding to herself as if there were no more applicable concept in the English language.

"Flaherty and me was happily married," Big Duck said. "'Til you come along." Flat got a smarty-pants smile on her face. This was the only part of the argument she liked. "I told Clinton you couldn't be saved."

"Saved," Tit said. "Between the two a you, I was never saved so much in my life."

Big Duck changed the subject. "We coulda left you in Hickman," he said. "We didn't have to befriend you. Who took care a you? When your time come, who found you shelter? With running water. And a working cookstove. Didn't even have to chop wood, did you, to build a fire. No, the wood was right there stacked up waiting for you. Not a light burning in a hundred miles in your time of need—and we put a roof over your head."

"A roof," Tit said. "Can't eat a roof. God forbid anybody around here should eat."

They were edging closer to the unspoken thing.

"Yer the one ruined it, you and that pharmacist, bringing her into the world," Big Duck said. Now he pointed his long straight preacher arm at me. "You two shoulda kept your word and got rid a her."

"That was no lie," Tit said. "We did try. Poor homely thing. Bet she wishes now we'd tried a little harder." Here it came. "Bringing her into this godforsaken place just to starve."

Big Duck's face turned white. A muscle in his cheek flexed spasmodically. "Now get this straight," he said. "No kid in my house ever starved." Silence rolled away from his untrue pronouncement in noisy waves that filled the shack. Any pronouncement that was true didn't need to be said ever, let alone once a week. *Starve* was the word. The boy on the ceiling starved to death. Little Duck and Jima both saw Tit carry the body out of the house and do something with it. Big Duck fell apart. It was his. He left Tit and Flat and didn't come back for two years.

The argument was over. Both Duck and Tit needed a drink. Tit reached into her cleavage. Big Duck gasped involuntarily, wishing it was his hand in there, not hers. She threw a bill on the table. "Bring it back sealed," she said. And he did.

—

Always quiet, never complaining, always at peace, never at odds, always resigned, never ambitious, always sad, never happy— the boy on the ceiling was back in the morning. Compared to him, Big Duck seemed hollow. Even when he was clean and combed, standing in bright sunshine in his white hat and his blue silk suit, Big Duck's face looked mottled and obscure, as if God was sick of him and was getting ready to paint him out of the family portrait. He seemed insubstantial and doomed, his soul a dark, receding blank. His bragging had no volume, his threats no force. It was this dark vision of him that—no matter how many times he humiliated me—forever made me regard him as a man who needed forgiveness. If the sight of me didn't grate on his nerves so much, I would have run over to give him his own best advice: "All things whatsoever ye would that men should do to you, do ye even so to them."

—

Kindness and stability we got from Iowa. Year after year, we three stood at the fence with Iowa surrounding us, dense and rich, fine and black, a sea of silt two hundred miles wide. We witnessed the succession of tasks, each with its own weather, its own season. It always began in spring with a distant report, the toylike sound of a tractor engine grabbing hold, ba-drum-drum-drum, bdrmmmmmmm. The tractor chugged methodically back and forth, delineating the vast sweep of land before us into perfect parallel rows. This was the great numbing labor of plowing. The plow turned over earth that was black as pitch, a solid black, a clean black, not the black of grime, of degradation or despair, but the alluvial black, the black of wealth, the black of oil.

Next came the anxiously timed tedium of planting, the wait for rain. Small green metal signs on the fence posts whispered the brand of the seed, but we couldn't read. The first bright green tender shoots seemed to arrive overnight, one per seed, rinsing the field in an indescribable tint, the color of a memory, a popped bubble. A few weeks went by, and tidy, organized fields of feed corn stretched to the horizon in every direction in even rows hundreds of yards long, straight and true, with no variation even where there was a slight inconsistency in the pitch of the terrain. Suddenly the corn was a foot high, then two feet, three feet, four.

Now came the endless cultivating between the long rows, the costly fertilizers applied in spurts from a great, poisonous drum. Now came the weed killers, the insecticides sprayed by crop dusters in lovely, heavy, brown, calligraphic jets on windless evenings at dusk. It was possible all this work would come to nothing. There could be a lack of rain or too much of it. A hailstorm during a delicate phase. A blight. An infestation of new weevils the chemists had not been introduced to before. With luck, the corn would grow taller than a man.

In the great, oppressive heat of late July, a wagonload of workers would arrive in the field. Straight through the white hot morning, straight through the brutal afternoon, boys and girls in bright hats and head scarves filled the rows, detasseling corn. Even I could see them. We stood at the fence, watching, silent, dusty, and barefooted, looking like children who didn't belong in public. It made us uncomfortable to see and hear boys and girls from town. With their white sneakers and gold wristwatches, their crushes and sunburns, we were glad to see them go. We welcomed the sight of the farmer rolling into the field alone on his massive harvester.

Finally the joyful ordeal everything depended on—the harvest. The farmer worked from first light straight through dusk. Sometimes he harvested in the dark, and we knew the next day it would rain. When all that plenty had been amassed and shipped to market, only stiff, dry, foot-high stalks were left in the fields, rasping paper-thin in the wind.

We were proud of our farmer. Only a severe man with a great heart for nature, a man willing to be small on a vast horizon, able to live life one row at a time, only a man who was physically strong, quietly measuring, emotionally renegade, who was willing to overlook all risk with modesty and stoicism, willing to find in work all that life offered—solace, fulfillment, sport, exercise, challenge, endurance, harmony, partnership, science, art, uncertainty—only that man was capable of such magnificent, epic submission to the weather and the soil. Farming was gambling disguised as discipline, godlessness disguised as hard work.

Autumn brought anxiety. We missed the sensible sound of the tractor out there in the field, chugging so ploddingly back and forth like Iowa's conscience. Lying beneath our tree in the noontime sun, looking straight up, Jima and me watched the fluttering orange and yellow leaves fill the whole sky like a ball of dancing flames purified of heat. We were cold. The boy on the ceiling was not always there. Smelling the musk of decay in the soil, I anticipated a time when he would float away for good. I was afraid I would be next.

We still had the train. We stood inside at the window each night, waiting for the 9:49.

—

Jima's yellow dress was gone. Now she wore Little Duck's hand-me-down Levi's, rolling up the cuffs. I was big enough for Levi's too. My cuffs we rolled up four times. Even so, they dragged in the dirt, fraying until only white threads were left—no blue. The thick wad of denim at my ankles chafed my skin and made me trip. Now, when we three stood at the fence watching the farmer farm, Jima and me looked like Little Duck's shadows. Jima with her messy, dirty ponytail was the long, loose, sidelong shadow of dusk. I was the squat headlong shadow of noon, crunched down to a third of its actual height by the foreshortening angle of the sun. I mentioned the math of our shadows to Jima. She gave me the *Shh* sign, a dusty finger up and down against her two sealed lips. She didn't want me saying anything too smart around here.

We were hungry. One itchy, damp, boiling summer day, we three ran away from home. We believed we could walk to town through the corn and be adopted. We crossed the railroad tracks and plunged down the steep bank. The runoff from the insecticide collected at the bottom of the ditch in a deadly, sludgy, fluorescent green stream. We jumped over it, getting some on us. It burned. We climbed up the other side of the bank to the field. Little Duck slipped under the fence, holding the barbed-wire strands up high for Jima and me so we could crawl under on our bellies. Jima stood up too soon and ripped a gash in her arm.

A sea of mature feed corn was neither restful nor calm. It was not benign. It was futuristic. It was menacing. The rows seemed miles long if you rode past in a wagon or an automobile. They snapped open and shut, endlessly swallowing you up and spitting you out, leaving you choking with agoraphobic panic. When you were walking, you were instantly disoriented. Furrows seemed to indicate rows, yet all sense of direction was lost. That was why they called it a sea. The intense, nasty, yellow-green color of the incessantly unfolding leaves, the aggressive upward thrust of their jointed stalks, evoked little of the marvel of growing things. Rather, they suggested the airless artificiality of a chemically dangerous, out-of-control science-fiction world under glass. The earth in the furrows between the rows was not solid. It was not even lightly tamped. To keep down weeds, it was cultivated. As such, it consisted of a soft, deep layer of small granules of soil. With every forward step, our bare feet sank six inches down into close, dusty, loose black dirt.

Little Duck was fast. He was strong and adept. We were holding him back. Our progress was agonizing. Jima's hair was all the way out of the clasp—the clasp was lost. She stopped to cry. Little Duck tried to turn back, but all the corn looked alike. We could see rows in every direction. We would drown here, we would die of exhaustion at the bottom of the endless sea of corn. Then they'd be sorry.

We were tempted to panic, but we had learned early in life that panic was bad for survival. We remembered our gut instincts. We turned our attention to the breathing of the sky, the small, moment-to-moment shifting of daylight, something we were good at. We caught the sun tick-tick-ticking ever so slightly east to west in the white, wet overhead light. This allowed Little Duck to establish south. South was where the railroad tracks lay. We followed him single file.

There was a low rumble in the sky. We hoped it was the only one, knowing nothing we ever hoped came true. There was another rumble. A thunderstorm. In mud we would be mired, yet we knew, somehow, not to rush, to just keep going. A low burst of silver brightness hit our eyes. It flashed hypnotically as we three trudged toward it. That brightness was the gleam of the sky glancing off the beautiful steel of the railroad tracks. We were on our way home. Let it rain.

Inside the shack, the crashing of Iowa thunder soothed our nerves from the soles of our feet to the crowns of our heads, filling us with the glory of a hundred trains at once. Clouds as big as the whole state went tearing through the sky north-northeast. The wind bent everything in its path. Rain whipped the wood of the shack so hard it would never be really dry again. We stood at the window, charmed by the storm. Flat was still muttering scripture. "And I heard a great voice out of the temple saying to the seven angels, Go your ways, and pour out the vials of the wrath of God upon the earth." Tit was still nodding out. They had never missed us, never knew we tried to run away from home. Now, they were missing the storm.

—

We accepted our plight. We stayed busy day and night, praying, choking down supplements, and translating maternal competition into love. Drifting aimlessly about our dirt yard, out to the fence, back to the tree, up to the tracks. Our faces were dirty. Our hands were dirty. Our minds were dirty too. We were those dirty people, doing things in a clump to kill time in a world of their own. When people got lost and drove by us by mistake, they didn't quite see us.

—

Our outhouse was full. I did a little exploring. I found a new shitting spot in the railroad ditch. I wanted to see what I did. I bent over to take a close look. I had accomplished something. I made a letter. It looked like the big *H* I saw in gold on the cover of our Holy Bible. I was impressed. I might be shitting scripture.

"Come here, you little shits." Tit called Jima and me inside. Gleaming and fluttering in some phosphorescent getup and a new red manicure, she unscrewed the lid from a great dark brown jar of brewer's yeast, new from Vita-Life's summer catalog. She stirred a heaping tablespoon of yeast into the tin cup. "This is ta boost yer immune system," she said, one eye on Flat. "Yer gettin' yer sixteen amino acids, plus fourteen minerals. Ya won't feel tired. You'll get yer proper rest at night, sleep like a baby. Ya got all the B vitamins ya need in here for yer nerves and yer digestion." Tit dealt in miracles now. Miracles were supposed to be rare occurrences, but the new Vita-Life catalog was full of them.

Eating yeast was like eating a rug. We learned to cheat. We carried the tin cup across the room and poured the contents out of sight, down our collars onto our chests. Even on our skin, it felt terrible. We wanted to run outside and rub it off as soon as

Tit turned her back, but Flat was hovering, waiting to snag us to undo the heresy.

"Only Christ offers life everlasting," Flat said. Her colorless eyes were narrower and beadier, her blue dress more threadbare. "For whosoever will save his life shall lose it: and whosoever will lose his life for my sake shall find it. For what is a man profited, if he shall gain the whole world and lose his own soul?"

We wanted to please her too. We both puked up a little something on the spot. We saw it, an actual smirk on Flat's face. "Run tell Tit the yeast has come up on you," she said. And run we did. But she was already gone.

—

It took years before I had a name for it, my mother's wavy, invisible pool of scent with its warm, mealy, tangy, yeasty, distilled, cured, alluring hint of comfort and eternity right here on earth. She took it with her when she tarted herself up to walk the streets of town, selling vitamins. It was not a smell I associated with safety, yet I wanted it near. I felt off balance without it. I tried to divert myself until she came back. Someone would drop her off somewhere. The front edge of her smell would find me, intruding on my consciousness. And here she came, walking across the railroad tracks in her high heels. A woman of mystery, taking her time, always taking her time. The word, when I finally did grow up and have a name for it, because I myself was up to my neck in the stuff, was *come*. My mother smelled like come—and not just her own, everyone's.

—

The boy on the ceiling was gone for good. For days, I looked for him in the rafters. Nights, I waited for him to come floating down to sleep, nestling his shoulders against mine. Instead Jima and me stared at each other, wide-eyed and grief-stricken. She gave me the *Shh* sign. He had stayed long enough to see us through. I couldn't believe I would never see him again. I looked for him everywhere.

—

The winter days were dim. The sun was pale. The extra darkness provoked fear. The cold numbed my toes and fingertips. I shivered, I wheezed. The frost etched our windows with bumpy spasms of complex indecipherable design, linked by cross-hatching of every type and angle, thick lines and thin, long and short, organic and geometric. There was a lot to study there, but I was too cold. My thoughts got stopped up with snot.

A light snow was welcome. It brightened the shack. Outside, it simplified the forms of things, revealing their structure. Each of the dormant cornfields stretching to the horizon was defined by the artful line of the barbed-wire fence, forming a huge yet tidy grid. The beautiful, shining, parallel steel lines of the railroad tracks swept east to west in an elegant arc, meeting at invisible points beyond.

But in snow, I couldn't get out to my shitting place. I went back to using the outhouse, where my shit got mixed up with everyone else's. I couldn't see what I did. It was cold in the shack, so cold we didn't move, which made it colder. We three stood by the stove, waiting for spring. All night, I listened to mice skittering randomly around the shack, nibbling and shredding whatever they could find. I heard our rat too. His sound was different. He knew what he wanted and where to get it. He waited for an opportunity, then he ran straight to it in a fast, direct, bulletlike raid.

One morning after a blizzard, all our windows were white. We were buried in twelve feet of snow. Snow had come down the chimney too. When Little Duck opened the woodstove to see why the fire was out, it was filled with snow. A lack of oxygen made me panic. I wished I lived in another place, a better place with better people where I could think all year. I stood by the stove in shame, hoping my rude wish didn't show on my face.

The hum of a tractor outside shocked us out of our trance. We three stood at the window, watching and listening. A shovel scraped snow off the glass. Our farmer was digging us out. "Praise the Lord," Flat said, taking the credit. Now *that* was offensive.

I'd never seen our farmer close-up before. His eyes were practical and spiritual, filled with strength, patience, cunning, and the wisdom of what to do in every weather. His nose was running. A tiny drop of snot glistened from the tip as he got back up on the tractor. He pushed the snowdrifts away from our front door with repeated, efficient sweeps of the plow blade. He knocked on our door. Big Duck, Tit, and Flat all shrank in the corner in shame. Little Duck opened the door. Our farmer was bringing us firewood, stacking it neatly by the stove. He did a double take, seeing only Little Duck, Jima, and me. "What happened to the fourth kid?" he said. The secret truth we couldn't even utter to ourselves was common knowledge. There were no secrets—that was the secret.

||

We heard a wall of sound approach, a
warlike, echoing, clackety rumble coming across the gravel pit.
I'd heard of the end of the world. This could be it. *Go your
ways and pour out the vials of the wrath of God upon the earth.*
Instead, lumbering steadily across the hard-packed, uneven,
gray floor of the pit, pulling the invisible wall of sound in its
wake, was a yellow earthmoving machine. Little Duck moved
in a trance toward the machine, grasping precisely what it
could and should do. He'd driven us up and down the dirt road
in Big Duck's roadster a few times, and now he wanted to drive
this. We watched the machine roll to a stop and idle in place,
shuddering so loud a duplicate idle echoed a mile away. Out
of the cab jumped a stocky, tan man, burly and athletic, with
a head of gleaming oily black curls. Black chest hair climbed
out of the open neck of his shirt. It was a knit shirt, jazzy and
casual, with red and yellow stripes across the front. It represented a world we'd never seen. The chain around the man's
neck was gold and braided, with no cross in sight. This was
Sam Fanelli, our first Italian.

Mr. Fanelli opened a survey and read it, then paced off a

length of ground. In the cab was a middle-aged, lard-legged, low-IQ killer. Mr. Fanelli signaled to him. The man put the machine in gear, chugged forward, and lowered the bucket, tooth-side down. We three sat beneath the tree to watch. The man stabbed and jabbed the hard-packed ground until it cracked. He turned the bucket right side up to scoop up dirt clods, stones, and dust. He chugged over to the rim of the pit, turning the bucket upside down to empty it. He did this a hundred times. Mr. Fanelli always waved him back to the next spot to dig, though that seemed obvious to us. A hole was a hole, nothing more.

We got so used to the echoing rumble that when it stopped our ears were shocked at the lack of it, shocked and a little bored with our own pathetic, machineless situation. Mr. Fanelli brought a lunch box over and sat with us under the tree. He smelled like aftershave, cotton, leather, and money. We smelled filthy and colorless. "Mind if I join you?" he said. The look on his face was lighthearted and clever, instantly causing us not to be strangers. Little Duck didn't know how to answer. What was the saucy thing a person said back to indicate consent?

"Yes sir," he said.

Mr. Fanelli sat down, opened the lunch box, and unfolded a sandwich wrapped in wax paper. Egg salad. He took a bite. Our eyes watered. He asked us our names. When I said mine, he looked at my forehead with sympathy.

"Crane," he said, "what happened to you?"

I said what they said. "My mother tried to get rid of me."

He stopped in mid-chew.

"You're not in school?" he said to Little Duck.

School. "No sir," Little Duck said. God the Father, Jesus

Christ Our Lord and Personal Savior, the Holy Spirit. The letters of Paul to the Corinthians. The Psalms of David. That was our school. Any other school was a tool of Satan.

"Your folks in there?" Mr. Fanelli said, nodding at our shack, which, from the look of things, was his shack.

Little Duck didn't know how to lie yet either. He used phrases from the argument too. Big Duck, he said, was hustling pool.

"Pool!" Mr. Fanelli said. "So your mother works?"

"Yes," he said. He should have stopped there, but he could see Mr. Fanelli wanted to hear more. "She's a whore."

"Christ, a whore!" The way Mr. Fanelli said it back to us revealed the harsh truth we worked so hard to deny: we had unusually terrible parents. Little Duck didn't mention Flat. It was incomprehensible to have a third useless parent doing the Lord's work from a piano stool on a diet of fingernails in a blue dress hanging from a safety pin.

We didn't know how old we were. Mr. Fanelli estimated our ages. Little Duck he figured as twelve, Jima ten, and me five. Mr. Fanelli told us he hailed from Chicago. He won the gravel pit, he said, in a poker game from the former pit boss, a crazy, drunken old Swede named Ole Briggs. Ole Briggs promised Mr. Fanelli the land had springs. Mr. Fanelli intended to find them. He took a bite. Chewing on one side of his mouth, he made a sweeping gesture across the horizon with his sandwich hand, a gesture that encompassed the dry, gray, gouged expanse of earth in the gravel pit. Little Duck's eyes accidentally followed the path of the egg salad sandwich through the air. "All this will be a beautiful lake by fall," Mr. Fanelli said. *All this a lake.* It was shocking to imagine this and shocking that he could talk and eat at the same time, so casually, as if there were always a sandwich to wave around. When we had food, the act of eating it rendered us silent. We three looked at each other and cracked very small smiles. We believed in Sam Fanelli in his jazzy striped shirt with his aftershave and his egg salad.

The next day, when Mr. Fanelli sat down under the tree with us and opened his lunch box, there were sandwiches in there for us. The bread was spongy and white and tasted like yeast. Between the two slices was fresh tuna salad made with real mayonnaise and a little chopped green olive. There was even a leaf of lettuce. We ate too fast. We ran up to the railroad tracks and threw up our sandwiches. After that day, we chewed slowly, one bite at a time, pausing between sandwich halves to allow our digestive systems to get used to having something to do.

Flat squealed. The next day when Mr. Fanelli was feeding us, the blue roadster came lunging over the railroad tracks. Big Duck climbed out and strutted down to the tree. He pulled a gun on Mr. Fanelli, asking him what the hell he thought he was doing, messing with his kids. It wasn't really us kids he was worried about. Big Duck didn't want Tit selling a vitamin to any new little foreign man with a lot of capital. Mr. Fanelli placed his half-eaten sandwich back in the lunch box. He wiped his lips with a paper napkin. He slowly rose to a standing position and there he stayed, his hands dangling at his sides, smiling, giving Big Duck time to stop acting stupid and start acting smart. But Big Duck was ranting about squatters' rights and the law of eminent domain. As he ranted, the killer rode over on the backhoe from the middle of the lake bed. He killed the engine, climbed down, and stood silently beside Mr. Fanelli.

"This is Lou," Mr. Fanelli said, gesturing to his thug.

Duck tried to back out of this without losing face. He offered the men a drink. "A drink," Mr. Fanelli said to Lou. "Now he wants to give us a drink." Lou laughed a laugh that was so short, it told you never to make him laugh again. Mr. Fanelli spit in Duck's face. They went back to work.

We'd never seen this before. It was kind of exciting. Now that we'd seen it done, we realized it was something we'd been wanting to do off and on for years.

—

The water was cloudy as it filled the lake bed. Mr. Fanelli said in ninety days the dirt would settle and the lake would be clear. "Watch these," he said, pouring two hundred bass fingerlings into the lake. "They'll be a foot long by fall." At the far end of the lake by the trees, Mr. Fanelli built a marina with a dock. Each morning, we awoke to the sound of his hammer ringing out across the water, echoing twice for every time the hammerhead hit the nail. *Make a joyful noise unto the Lord.* Surely this was it! We ran down to the shore to watch him work. His forearms were strong, his eyes and hands worked together methodically and in harmony. His features were humble yet proud as he concentrated on what he was doing. He never sweated. Instead, his black wavy hair glowed, his arms shone. He asked Little Duck to hand him things, a hammer, a nail, a board.

When the dock was done, Mr. Fanelli built a bait shop in the shade by the trees. He brought in a plumber to do the plumbing and an electrician to do the electricity. The killer was long gone. These were regular Iowans. They had tattoos and some teeth were missing, but they had never strangled anyone.

In ninety days, the water *was* clear. We could see the summer sky reflected in it, sharp as a mirror, just as Mr. Fanelli said we would. Down at the bottom, darting like dark impulses, were the bass. They'd doubled in size and tripled in number since they were introduced. "What's your advice?" he said to us. "Should I name the lake Lake Ole after the Swede or Lake Mary after my mother?"

"Lake Mary," we said. It was easier to remember and easier to say. We felt important. No one had ever invited us to name something before.

Mr. Fanelli hired Little Duck to be bait boy. Jima and me followed him down the shore of the lake to work, Jima slipping sidelong in his shadow, me charging headlong, my eyes in a squint. We dug for night crawlers. When men came to fish, we were there, ready and waiting with worms. They carried their tackle boxes out to the boats. They tipped their hinged outboard motors into the water. A rip of the rip cord and the engines purred alive in the soft morning air. Off they went, motoring peacefully across the lake in different personal directions to fish. When they came back, they told us where the fish were in voices that were calm and reasonable. We listened in awe as they commented back and forth about the world, the Cold War, the Korean conflict, FHA mortgages, the housing boom, things that were printed in newspapers we never saw. We began to feel deceived by the evangelists who raised us. Other people were not standing around in the dirt all day, getting their only ideas from different books of the Bible.

In the bait shop, Mr. Fanelli kept the radio tuned to KIOA, Iowa's most popular Top 40 radio station. We listened in awe to our first rock and roll. Other people weren't standing around the dirt all day singing hymns. I was proud of Jima—she was good at remembering the words. Little Duck and me would crack up when she lip-synced Fats Domino:

> You made (dum-dum)
> me cry, (dum-dum)
> When you said (dum-dum)
> Good-bye. Ain't that a
> Shame. (Ba-dum ba-dum ba-dum ba-dum)
> Oh my tears fell like
> Rain. (Ba-dum ba-dum ba-dum ba-dum)

One evening, Mr. Fanelli invited us to try out his new motorboat. He filled it with gasoline. A little bit spilled, causing rainbows to spool out on the water, evaporating delightfully, leaving that delicious, cheerful smell of horsepower hanging in the air. We climbed into the boat, laughing out loud at how insecure we felt, wobbling as the curve-bottomed boat reacted to our unsteady new weight. Little Duck pulled the rip cord, his face uncommonly pleased at the sound of the motor's jillion timed explosions. When Mr. Fanelli roared out across the water, the back end of the boat left a beautiful row of V-like waves flowing out behind it like a bride's train. We swirled around the lake, bumping across our own wake so hard we couldn't stop laughing.

Afterward, we sat on the dock with Mr. Fanelli while he smoked a cigar. Loose, free, unfretful companionship—with a man who told the truth, who gave us sandwiches without hurting our pride, who spit in the eye of our corrupt, divided father. We loved Mr. Fanelli more than life itself. We looked up at the stars, dreaming of Chicago.

—

What was water, anyway? It rolled around in its lake bed like any liquid. On misty summer mornings, it made a white blanket of vapor between itself and the sky. The wind turned it into a third thing I couldn't explain, shattering it into a billion dancing points. I dipped in my hand and felt it, satisfied and mystified.

—

Each day Little Duck washed down the rowboats, cleaned slime off the oars and outboards, bleached life jackets, hosed the dock, worked the cash register. Mr. Fanelli taught Little Duck to tinker with engines, taking them apart, cleaning them, putting them back together again. He gave Little Duck his old white cotton dress shirts when the buttons were missing and there were holes in the elbows. Little Duck ripped the sleeves off at the shoulder seam and wore the shirts open. Now when he went loping down to the bait shop in the morning, his white dress shirt flapping in the sunlight, his golden chest peeking through, his hair swept back in long waves, he looked sharp. Jima and me drifted along in his wake. We wanted white shirts too.

We learned to fish. Mr. Fanelli lent us an old rowboat. Little Duck repaired a discarded engine for us. It purred into action when he pulled the rip cord. It's one thing to see fishermen docking their boats in the marina after a day of fishing, showing each other the fish they've caught—and another thing to witness the dying of a fish yourself.

Little Duck took us out to the shady spot beneath the trees where everyone said the fish were. I imagined the fish resting down there in their shady hole, watching the big bottom of our boat arrive at the top of their water the way night arrived for us in our earthly sky. We dropped anchor. I imagined the fish watching the rusty, mossy, curved iron T come falling slowly on its rope through their heavens down to their soft, sludgy earth. *Plop.* The anchor displaced its weight in mud, sending a cloud of it spilling mightily upward, diffusing slowly into the water.

Little Duck threaded an earthworm over the hook on my fishing pole. I'd been digging them up for weeks, and the life of a worm interested me. The way they went wriggling through the soil in the pail, not seeming to notice whether or not they were sliding over each other, made me wonder if they knew they were in a pail at all. Did they have memory? Did they remember a time when they were still in the ground? Did they have sensation? Did my worm dislike the dry brightness of the air when Little Duck lifted it out of the soil to bait the hook? Did the hook hurt? The way fishermen insisted a worm never felt anything made me think the worm definitely did. How did water feel to the worm now as I lowered it into the lake? How did it feel to get bitten by a fish? Were worms able to prepare their worm babies for life as a worm, telling them what to expect and what to avoid? If worms had knowledge, I suspected it was the kind that was useless.

We waited with our lines in the water, our baited hooks dangling there like fish sandwiches. Our arms felt cool in the green shade of the trees. Little Duck got a bite. As in everything he did, Little Duck reacted gracefully, with a natural understanding of the mechanics involved, of the process and the reward. He set the hook, making the fish mad. We all three watched as his line went flying off the reel, zinging out over the surface of the lake. It stopped. The fish was taking a break, resting a moment. Little Duck reeled hard, drawing the fish closer and closer. Jima and me watched the water. Like magic, a fish-shaped slice of darker water seemed to approach us a few feet below the surface, brightening ever so subtly as it got closer, until right beside the boat it turned into a living, breathing silver thing awkwardly stuck to Little Duck's hook. While Jima and me were entranced with this, other fish were eating the worms off our loose, dangling hooks. Neither of us felt even so much as a tremor in our poles. Little Duck leaned over the side with a net and scooped the lovely, silver, furious thing into the bottom of our boat. We sat there watching the fish stop breathing. His sides pumped furiously, his gills opened and closed, his eyes bugged out. Air, which was life to us, was death to him. *Oooooooooooooooo.*

———

When fishing season was over, Mr. Fanelli went home to Chicago. He wouldn't be back until March. We couldn't live without him, but we had to. We focused on his lake until spring came. The first sight of his truck, the first sound of his hammer ringing across the lake—they were cause for joy. We ran down to the bait shop, light on our feet.

Mr. Fanelli had big plans. Housing was desperately needed in Iowa. He intended to build central Iowa's first man-made lake community. He let us watch. We stood in the shade of the trees by the bait shop all day, enthralled. Men rolled in on yellow machines to excavate basements and grade yards. They scraped a beautifully banked road around the shore. We three looked at each other, cracking very small smiles. We'd never found our way to town. Town had found its way to us.

Instead of building one house at a time, Mr. Fanelli built thirty-five at a time, saving the biggest and best for himself. Crews of men moved right down the shore from lot to lot, completing each stage. In ninety days, we had a neighborhood. Some of the fishermen told Mr. Fanelli while he was at it, to knock down our shack. Jima and me were standing in the shade of the trees when we heard that. We shivered. We stepped closer together, our sides completely touching, so we would take up less room. "They're not hurting anybody," Mr. Fanelli said.

He sent for Mrs. Fanelli, his blonde, lasagna-making wife, and Mercy, their sullen, eleven-year-old, dark-haired daughter. We studied Mercy for signs of the gratitude and enlightenment that surely came with having such a man for a father, a house-builder, a lake-digger, but Mercy was miserable. The only thing that made her eyes light up was Little Duck. She followed him around the bait shop, holding things he asked her to hold, handing him things he asked her to hand him, giving us the strange impression that she would be happier if she were one of us.

We stood in the shade of the trees, watching as people began to move into the houses. We felt sorry for them. They lived so far away from the solid truths of this place, the stark history. They lived on the tippy-top of the surface, with no connection to what happened before. They would never know the way the wind sifted grit down on your skin all day when there was no lake here, just a pit from a played-out gravel mine. They turned the handle of a faucet and water poured out. They would never know the real mechanics of water, how you had to prime the pump by cranking the handle a couple of times to remove the air from the pipe so it would pull water up out of the aquifer—gushing, tangy, and silver—right into your tin cup. They wouldn't know what it meant to depend on the train, beginning with the feeling in the soles of your feet of the wheels on the tracks twenty miles away, and ending with that great, chilling, two-tone chord as sixty loaded railroad cars poured past. They would know nothing of this, feel nothing of this. All of their knowledge, all of their feelings related only to the things they brought with them, much of it new, to a "place" that was itself brand-new, a place that wasn't deep and wasn't wide. It consisted only of a new layer of shiny building materials hammered together, reflecting the sun with toylike insignificance. But they didn't know they didn't know. In yet another way, we were invisible.

—

The children of Lake Mary went to school that fall on a yellow bus. We had somewhere to go too—the bait shop was open all year. Mr. Fanelli installed an antenna on the roof. We saw our first television. He built a beautiful bar out of varnished wood and lined up bar stools with red leather seats. Now we had liquor. When Mr. Fanelli wasn't looking, Jima sipped capfuls of whisky. Next, Mr. Fanelli got a cigarette machine. We slipped our night-crawler quarters into the slot and bought a pack of Winstons. We smoked Winstons because we liked the jingle. "Win-ston tastes good like a (clap-clap) cigarette should." Mr. Fanelli brought his old magazines down to the bar. Now we had *Life*.

All winter the fishermen sat at the bar, talking about the fish they'd caught in summer. We got to know their names and their personal problems. When they were gone, Jima and me sat at the bar with our feet dangling, thumbing through *Life*. We looked at the food. Bologna. Dill pickles. American cheese. Small, bright yellow, bite-sized cubes of Velveeta were shown piled in a pyramid on a round platter, each with a toothpick stuck in the middle of it. Ritz crackers were fanned out in a circle around the edge of the platter. For people to have enough food to play with like that seemed un-Christian. We forgave them. We were happy there with the beautiful bottles all lined up on the wall, the red neon B-A-R sign flashing in the window overlooking the lake.

—

It was a bright, bracing May day. Clouds raced each other across the sky, ducking when they came to the sun. We were busy with worms again. We felt confident and capable. We'd gotten through the winter easily with the bait shop open. Now Mr. Fanelli was building a beach. We watched in awe as a hundred tons of sand were gently poured from a tipping dump truck into pyramids evenly spaced along the shore of Lake Mary. Men raked the sand flat and smooth. Mr. Fanelli made sure the beach included us. The men poured sand right under our tree. They raked it deep and smooth.

With sand, Jima came into her own. That shy, apologetic, stiff little thing with the crooked teeth, the long, dirty hair half out of the clasp, the slanted gray eyes, twisting her shoulders away from life, slipping sidelong out of the fray, turned bossy. She had a vision. She built a beautiful ancient Biblical land out of sand that she called "The Land of Ablah-Dablah." Jima determined the order of things, always beginning with the mountain made by her. She packed hard and was completely consistent. She had learned: if she didn't pack hard or wasn't consistent, the mountain would collapse when Little Duck dug the tunnel under it. A few times she'd tried to dig the tunnel herself. Her arms were too short. Little Duck's shoulder was double-jointed. His muscles were coordinated. He dug the tunnel deep, right down to the dirt, and narrow—that was the key. A narrow tunnel was not as likely to bring the mountain down. He dug it in halves, hoping to make the ends meet under the mountain. We held our breath when he dug the second half. We waited, we watched for that moment when he was up to his shoulder in sand and he smiled—it meant he could feel his fingers wiggling free deep under the mountain.

On top of the mountain, Jima made a lovely temple with a dome like the illustration in our Bible. For the dome, she scooped up wet sand with Mr. Fanelli's discarded ice cream scoop. The stair steps leading down to the town she made with a ruler. We loved to watch her, slicing for the risers, scraping for treads.

My turn. I combed our land with a broken comb, forming carefully pointed dunes and wavy desert plains without destroying anything we'd built. We had learned that I should keep my knees back out of the way, and that I should reach with my elbow held high. When we were done, we sat back on our heels, feeling the hot sun on our arms, entranced with our land.

And then we'd watch our land decay. A seed from our tree, a twig, would drift down and land on the mountain. A bird would come peck at that. The tunnel would cave in. The wind would blow rounded corners onto my dunes. It would rain. Everything would become dented, eroded, and crushed. And we understood what had happened to all those glorious places in the Bible. They too had decayed.

———

Mr. Fanelli installed a grill in the bar. Now the neon sign flashing in the window overlooking the lake said *BAR* in red, *& GRILL* in blue. He hung a little black menu board on the wall and lined up white letters to tell the fishermen what he would cook. How we envied them, being able to read and to order whatever they felt like.

"I'll have a hamburger."

"I'll have a hot dog with chili, no onions."

When no one was looking, we went through the garbage. The leftovers were delicious—hamburgers, cheeseburgers, sausage with peppers. On slow days or rainy days, when no one fished and the men who came into the bait shop wanted to drink, not eat, there wasn't any garbage. When Mr. Fanelli wasn't looking, we would each eat a spoonful of Heinz ketchup, careful not to reduce the level of the bottle too much. If there wasn't enough ketchup for all three of us to have a spoonful, one of us would lick the glass threads of the ketchup bottle clean, the other would lick the inside of the white cap. Heinz ketchup, we knew, was the best ketchup, because Heinz had 57 varieties.

Jima snuck whisky, one small slurp at a time. We loved the orderly cigarette machine with its choice of brands, its simple mechanics. In went the quarter. We listened to it roll down the chute. When the machine knew for sure it was a quarter, you'd pull the throttle under the pack you wanted and it would slip softly down into the tray.

There was a black wall phone behind the bar. "If that's for me, I'm not here," the fishermen would say when it rang. Mr. Fanelli would answer it and lie for them. We knew their complete histories by then, listening from the corner of the bar or the shadows of the trees outside, but they didn't know us. When they paid us for night crawlers, twenty-five cents a quart, they didn't quite see us. If they did, they saw my deformity. "What's wrong with her?" they asked Mr. Fanelli in front of me. Mr. Fanelli would smile as if they'd be better off asking what was wrong with themselves.

"Birthmark, I guess," he'd say.

Some of the fishermen thought they'd seen a rat up by our shack. They recommended that Mr. Fanelli call the Board of Health to see if our shack should be condemned. Jima and me would shiver when they said that. I would look over at Little Duck, crouching in the shadows of the trees, cleaning the parts of an outboard motor with kerosene. He kept doing whatever he was doing as if he didn't care, but I could see from the way his shoulder blades lay in his back that his feelings were hurt. "They're not hurting anybody," Mr. Fanelli would say.

Sometimes after Mr. Fanelli closed the bait shop and all the men of Lake Mary had gone home, we'd take out our boat. Little Duck would swing the rudder wildly from left to right, throwing the boat from side to side and us with it. The flak made beautiful waves. He'd steer back over them fast and hard, bumping the prow against the head of each wave with an echoing crack. We loved to feel the lake water splashing on our arms in the dark night air. *We have a right to be here*, our boat was saying. But when we walked back home along the shore road, we were dejected, wondering what would become of us.

—

That food began as a living thing and ended up as fecal matter upset me. That hamburger was a cow. That hot dog was a pig. When we ate such a thing, it disappeared and became us. The only by-products were gas and waste. How could this be? I found a private, spacious shitting place down by the railroad bridge where the reeds were tallest and straightest. My accomplishments grew more complex. *S*, *Se*, *Ni*—based on what I'd seen in *Life*, I was shitting advertisements. I wished that I could read.

—

One oppressive summer afternoon, I was out in my spot in the reeds, squatting there with my jeans at my ankles and the sweat drying on my arms. I was making *He*, when I heard a combination of snickers and silence that wanted to be snickers. Jump Wicket and Radley Stokes plunged down the railroad bank, wielding sticks. Thin, blond, and heartless, with dead, blue eyes, Jump was Lake Mary's notorious bully. He came by his sadism honestly: his personality was a blank; his boredom pathological. His sidekick, Radley, was shorter and rounder, with freckles the size of ladybugs across his cheeks. Radley had to work at his sadism, the way dull people work at an enthusiasm of any type. His motivation was fear. He was Jump's original victim.

These two rode their bikes around Lake Mary all day looking for kids to intimidate. Then they retreated to hideouts where they could indefinitely wait out any attempts at recrimination by parents. One of their hideouts was our inlet. Where the shore road ended, they wheeled their bikes into the reeds, lay them down flat, and climbed up to sit on the railroad bank. Here they remained without detection, overlooking the innocent little harassed community in which they lived. It was inevitable. It was only a matter of time before they'd be hiding in their hiding place when I came out to shit.

When you're being coerced, you notice everything human and inhuman about your sadist's face, timing, and mannerisms. The slightest flexing of the muscles of the face beneath the skin speaks volumes to you in terms of predicting what will come next—freedom or more pain. For Jump, torturing me brought a sexual release. The intensity of his attention, his sensitivity in choosing a method, his obvious pleasure in the flood of hormones I must have excreted as discomfort led to helplessness, helplessness led to shame, shame led to fear, and fear to pain—the entire transaction was like a reverse seduction—the attention was there, but the love was negative. There was a concavity in Jump's chest that suggested he was missing a whole range of emotions. The way he sat down and took charge of me, ordering me to do this or that, showed he'd thought this out, planning commands that would make me feel powerless. I did whatever he told me to, diverting my mind by noticing small things about him, like the fact that both of his sneakers were ripped in the same place, along the big toe where his feet were trying to grow. The knit neckline of his T-shirt was stretched out in an unbecoming oval. Radley's clothes were all new. He overfilled them, being plump. He stood there, watching Jump torture me, with mild general curiosity, killing time by tearing the head of a cattail to bits. Radley did have in his chest the full set of moral emotions a person was supposed to be issued at birth, but he chose to ignore them.

It goes without saying that a sadist first makes you undress. Naked people are at a huge disadvantage. I had an additional problem. My ribs pressed hard against my dirty skin, showing I was unfed. My belly was distended. My legs were bowed and too short for my big disfigured head. I stood there ashamed. There were unsavory tasks that Jump liked to watch me do involving my accomplishment. I was to stamp on it in my bare feet. I did. Now I was to smear it on my cheeks. I did. Next, eat some. This was not the worst thing that could happen. In waste, there was still nourishment. I later learned that people lost in boats at sea with no provisions drank their own urine. They chewed their own leather belts and ate their own feces. Waste was food that had been beaten up, used up, broken down. It was food in its most exhausted form, acidified, alkalized, fermented, mashed. It could not be integrated. But sometimes, compared to everything else in sight, it was still food.

"Now, hit her," Radley said afterward, but Jump never did. Hitting didn't interest him. He made me do things that were not polite. Yes, things like that. The muscles around his lips would distort themselves as he got worked up. During this, something appalling occurred. Against my will, I became fond of Jump's smell. I snapped. I pretended we were in love.

—

Tit went macrobiotic on us. She boiled brown rice. The new fall Vita-Life catalog was full of it. She sat Jima and me down at the table and made us both eat three-quarters of a cup. We had to chew each mouthful fifty times. We weren't supposed to swallow until our rice had turned to paste. Once Tit had inspected us and drifted away, we ran to the sink to spit out the disgusting slurry.

Flat pounced. If Tit could go macrobiotic, Flat could go Pentecostal. She made us testify. She called on the Holy Spirit to enter us both. We couldn't leave until we had demonstrated one of His gifts—prophecy, healing, preaching, prayer, interpretation, or glossolalia. We both chose glossolalia. A spewing coil of vowels with a sprinkling of diphthongs, and who was to say we weren't speaking in tongues? Jima got pretty good at it. She spun in place. She rolled around the floor. She learned to make her body shake and jerk. We both rolled our eyeballs back into our heads and fluttered the lashes, chanting nonsense. Whirling, spinning, shaking, quaking, chanting, humming—it was fun to induce ecstasy. All you needed for ecstasy was a little momentum and a little imagination—and one of your mothers saying you had to demonstrate the presence of the Holy Spirit in your life if you ever wanted to go down to the bait shop again.

—

"Jailhouse Rock," "Peggy Sue," "Whole Lotta Shakin' Goin' On." We heard it on the radio all winter. We saw it on TV—twisting, jitterbugging, doing the stroll. Jima, that shy, apologetic, stiff little thing, came out of her shell to rock and roll. Demonstrating the presence of the Holy Spirit in her life had made her limber. Liquor made her bold.

—

As soon as the weather was warm, we returned to the sand. This year when we built the Land of Ablah-Dablah, the

Tanner brothers rode their tricycles up the shore road to watch. They were dying to play in the sand with us, but they weren't allowed. They would sit on their trikes, hands on the handlebars, one foot on the sidewalk, watching. Their Doberman would bound over and sniff my behind, wagging his tail madly as if to say, *All clear*. One day, the Tanner brothers broke their parents' rule. They risked severe punishment by sneaking along the railroad tracks to us, their pockets loaded with sand toys that would add to our shimmering, epic creation.

Bobby was the older Tanner. He was all business, packing wet sand into a Dixie cup, turning it upside down twenty times to make a village of little Biblical houses. Cooper was the younger Tanner. He had a large, lovely head, daydreaming brown eyes, and a sweet, husky voice. He landscaped. When he stuck a hundred green pine needles around our government building to make a lawn, a little tremor formed in the back of my throat. To make our lake, he filled a rusty cake pan with lake water, then surrounded it with reeds. I went with him to collect reeds from the inlet. In clusters of five or six, he stuck the reeds along the rim of the pan to create an aquatic effect. Then, and only then, everyone sat back on their heels and watched as the remainder of our land was combed into expert, rolling, windswept dunes by me.

—

We heard it at the bait shop first. The pharmacist's wife left him. He was selling his house in town and moving out to Lake Mary. Little Duck and Jima both looked at me. For once I had something to run home and tell my mother. She listened to me for the first time in eight years. A dewy, fresh look enveloped her features, a look I'd never seen. Her lips were soft and supple, gently turned up at the corners; her eyes were childlike, anticipating happiness and escape. Could it be she loved someone, and that someone was my father?

Sight unseen, the pharmacist bought the empty lot next to our shack, the lot that no one wanted because we were trash. One sullen, humid afternoon, he drove out to look at it. The word *pharmacist* made me expect a man who was tall, thin, and busy. He wasn't. He was a jumpy, lumpy, destroyed man with poor vision. Our big heads were the same shape, only his forehead wasn't deformed. I heard the brainy, mathematical mood of him. It was deeply familiar. It was my own. I studied his face—our face. I wanted to know him, but he scrambled his features to discourage that. He was on edge and it made me nervous. He walked around the lot stoop-shouldered in a huge, dumb, short-sleeved shirt with his hands in his pockets and his big head thrown back, looking at the sky instead of the land. It was difficult to imagine such a man captivating a slut like Tit with conversation. There was no accounting for human attraction.

Mr. Fanelli built the pharmacist a Cape. Jima and me ran home from the bait shop often to watch. Tit watched too, leaning in the window, sweet with perfume. Big Duck was furious at Tit's happiness. He watched her closely, his face brittle and chalk-white with the special pain that erotic obsession inflicts on the brain. "Don't you be going over there," he'd say to Tit. "When he moves in."

"Why would I go over there?" Tit would say. "I don't got no business over there. I got everything I want right here."

The first leaves were falling from our tree, floating in great swinging zigzags down to the sand the day the moving van came. Men jumped out and carried a sofa, a bed, and a plaid reading chair into the pharmacist's house. The minute Big Duck left, Tit went over there. She went inside with love on her face and came back out with more. When Big Duck came home, he noticed the change in her. "You went over there, didn't you," he said.

"I go where I want and I do what I want," Tit said. "I don't gotta answer to you."

One cold afternoon I peeked into the pharmacist's bedroom window. He and Tit lay on his bed with their foreheads touching, their drugs beside them on the spread. They were talking. I was thrilled at the sound of his voice. I recognized him from my watery time in the womb. We had walked the dull streets of town together, my mother and me, always ending up at his house when his wife wasn't home. I forgave them for trying to get rid of me. I decided that the love these two felt for each other overlapped, accidentally, with love for me.

Sometimes when the pharmacist was inside, sitting in his plaid chair watching television, something came over me. Instead of heading out to the reeds to make my accomplishment, I would tiptoe over to his garage and leave a small token of my existence in the cool darkness by the open door. I knew without having to look which letter I'd produced. It was always *O*.

Tit was too happy. She was too calm. Big Duck took it out on me.

I was wearing the red cowboy hat given to me by Mr. Fanelli. It was made of felt with a rawhide chin tie. It fit perfectly. No one had claimed it from the lost and found down at the bait shop. The sight of me with a hat burned Big Duck up. He called me to his knee. I was going on nine years old, too old to be his fool, but I didn't know how to say so. "Let me see that

hat," he said. "Is that a Stetson?" He lifted the hat off my head and turned it upside down. He tilted the inside toward him so he could read the label. "Made in Japan," he said. He was a little less envious. "Isn't that hat too small?" It wasn't—it fit just right—but I was afraid to contradict him. I played dumb, nodding enthusiastically.

"I'll fix it for you if you want me to," he said. "Do you want me to fix it, so it's not too small?"

He was looking at me, his glittering black eyes intent on me and me alone, smiling right at me and me alone. Tit and Flat were watching, getting ready to laugh.

He placed the hat in his lap and took out a pocketknife. He cut a gash in the brim over the right ear, another gash over the left. That didn't look right, but I didn't say anything. "There," he said. He put it on my head. Instead of coming to rest above my forehead like it used to, the hat slipped down my nose, covering my eyes. The tops of my ears stuck out through the gashes like little fleshy sex organs you aren't supposed to see. They all laughed.

Inside the hat I turned red. "You can see, can't you?" he said, baiting me. I nodded, the big, loose, red brim flopping *yes*. Jima was watching, her slanted gray eyes speckled and furious. "You like it like that, don't you?" Big Duck said. I nodded again, the brim flopping. "Go play," he said. I ran into the wall. Our parents laughed, enjoying themselves.

Big Duck went down to the pool hall. Tit went next door to see the pharmacist. Jima and me studied my ruined hat. "Don't you worry, Crane," she said. "We're going to fix it back the way it was, only better." She had the drunkard's meaningless sincerity, persuasively pledging things that could never be.

Frilly yellow daffodils and fat pink tulips burst forth from Mrs. Fanelli's flower bed. Similarly, over the winter, Mercy had become voluptuous. She was now a sultry girl with heavy periods and a faint dusting of facial hair above the lips. She wore full skirts, Capezio flats, and white blouses bleached to God-like purity, unbuttoned to the third button to show teenage cleavage, collars turned up in back, cuffs rolled up to the elbow. From the beginning, Mr. Fanelli had encouraged Little Duck to befriend his bratty, difficult daughter. In the hundreds of tasks required to build and maintain the beautiful world of Lake Mary, this was Mr. Fanelli's single error. For three years, Mercy had followed Little Duck around, holding things he asked her to hold, handing him things he asked her to hand him. Now Mercy and Little Duck were in love.

"If you so much as touch her, you're dead," Mr. Fanelli said to Little Duck.

"Yes sir," Little Duck said.

Little Duck was quiet, graceful, and intense, his hair swept back in long waves, his tan chest winking out at you under his white dress shirt. At night, he walked into town along the railroad tracks to pay for sex with Dolly, a happy-go-lucky destitute woman who lived in a blue trailer on the town line. Still, when he went loping down to the bait shop in the morning, pink and gold stars swirled around his head if Mercy came near. He kept doing whatever he was doing, but his jaw softened with emotion. All day in the corners of his mouth, he nursed the image of what she was wearing. His way of loving without social expectation was to let his desire for Mercy blend into his being like invisible health.

"Are you going to marry Mercy?" we would ask him when she had left the bait shop for the day.

He kept doing whatever he was doing. He took a long time to answer, so we knew how much he wanted to. "Nah," he said. "I'll be lucky if I see her naked." He named his boat MMM-GOOD, copying the letters in the Campbell's Soup ad. He bought the decals, gold letters with a black shadow, and applied them to the stern. Everyone who saw it sang the Campbell's jingle. Jima and me cracked very small smiles. We knew who the three *M*s really stood for.

Did he touch her? Something happened. Mr. Fanelli caught someone doing something. He fired Little Duck. Now Little Duck walked into town in the morning along the railroad tracks. He pumped gas at a gas station. He worked on cars. Half the time he stayed in town overnight. Mercy stayed home. At night, the light in her upstairs bedroom window burned low. We could see it across the lake, both the real thing and its soft, bobbing reflection.

—

Now it was just Jima and me down at the bait shop, digging for worms. Some new fellow hosed down the dock. When we came home to the shack, Flat smelled liquor on Jima's breath. She smelled smoke in our hair. We didn't care. She sat at the piano and called us to worship. We didn't go. She threatened us, hissing Revelation. "And there appeared another wonder in heaven, and behold a great red dragon," she would say with a shrill, scratchy nastiness that could have passed as provocation to assault. "Having seven heads and ten horns, and ten crowns upon his heads. And his tail drew the third part of the stars of

heaven and did cast them to the earth." Her voice scraped at
our nerves, but we were no longer afraid. "And upon her forehead," Flat would hiss, trying to scare us with the harlot part,
"was a name written, MYSTERY BABYLON THE GREAT, THE MOTHER
OF HARLOTS AND ABOMINATIONS OF THE EARTH."

Now when Tit called us to the table for brown rice, we didn't
go. The rice would stay in the pan for weeks, producing an
interesting beer smell and a slick white bacteria. Our mothers
were losing their grip on us. Too bad—they had their chance.

—

Just when we least expected it, Big Duck had a new look on
his face: respect. When he tuned in the radio church service
on Sunday, his glittering black eyes were chastened. His lips
were solemn and sincere. The voice of a new preacher from
Oklahoma filled the shack. Dr. Paige Jiggins was building a
powerful reputation as a charismatic broadcaster. Dr. Jiggins
was seeking pilgrims to come and help him found Christ Town,
Oklahoma, a town with its own television station. He wanted
followers who were dedicated to getting in on the ground floor.
His message was one of prosperity. His voice was cocksure,
hypnotic, and indignant. God didn't mean for those who loved
him to be poor. Neither did Christ. And least of all did the
Holy Spirit. The Holy Spirit wanted us to prosper. The true
Christ wanted nothing more than to bless us in proportion as
we blessed ourselves.

"Who comes forward now to be blessed?" Dr. Jiggins said.
A man in the radio audience rolled up to the microphone in a
wheelchair. We all heard the man say he'd been confined to a
wheelchair for twenty-seven years with a debilitating muscle

ailment. Dr. Jiggins laid hands on the cripple. He asked the radio audience to join him in praying for a complete healing. As we listened, the man rose up out of the wheelchair and walked. A complete healing had occurred. Frenzy seized the radio audience. There were shrieks of joy, wild clapping, and an impromptu chorus of "Glory, Glory, Hallelujah."

"That old trick," Tit said.

But Big Duck was hooked. "Say," he said to Tit, holding his white hat by the brim with both hands, leaning forward submissively on the chair, his dark eyes pleading the way they did at the end of the argument. "We could try again. He needs pilgrims. We still got it in us—you do, I do. Whaddya say we blow this dump and go to Oklahoma? Get in on the ground floor?"

Jima and me listened from the corner. There was no mention of us. Flat chewed her fingernails down to the skin. There was no mention of her.

Tit looked out our window at the pharmacist's house. "It don't rain enough in Oklahoma for me," Tit said. That was all she said, though Big Duck kept watching her and waiting. His dark eyes were crushed.

———

Something was going wrong next door. There was some kind of episode involving a hospital. The pharmacist sat in his plaid chair all spring watching TV. Tit still went over there, but she didn't stay as long. When it was warm, the pharmacist came out and sat in his lawn chair once again.

He looked distraught. His face began to twist in two separate directions. Both directions were under pressure. Without darkness, Big Duck had always told us, there would be no light.

But looking at the pharmacist, it seemed to me that for some souls this was not the case. For some souls, without darkness, there would be no darkness.

Everyone saw the pharmacist sitting in his lawn chair and thought he was still there, just a little tired or not feeling particularly well, but he wasn't. He was beyond all that. He was already a refracted thing, already a remembered thing. Reality was out of his reach. When he turned around to refer to it, it wasn't where he left it. It had dissolved. His resolve to refer to it dissolved too. Sometimes he stayed in his lawn chair all night, wide awake. If I woke up, I went to the window to see if he was sitting there. And he always was, the whites of his eyes patrolling the lake, the lawn, the summer sky in great mad arcs, as if every sound of nature were magnified, echoing, insidious, and personal.

—

It was a perfect day for building the Land of Ablah-Dablah. The hot spell was over. A light rain the evening before had made the sand easy to mold. The pharmacist was sitting in his lawn chair when the Tanner brothers snuck over with their tools. We knelt together in the sand to build our land. Jima made the mountain. Bobby dug the tunnel. He made the Biblical village, packing the wet sand into the Dixie cup. We sat back on our heels to watch Cooper landscape. He stuck pine needles into the lawn around the government building. He planted the juniper sprigs. He was inserting a reed when our land blew up. All the sand went flat. The explosion rang in our ears for years—so close, so loud, so long that it echoed around the lake three times while it was still exploding.

We ran next door into the sound. We had no choice—it pulled us to it as if it were lateral, invisible quicksand. The air around us was thick and elastic with time; we saw light waves bending in it. We saw the pharmacist bending in it. He sat tipped over backward in his green metal lawn chair. His face was gone. His brains looked like eight or nine raw chickens steaming in the grass. There was a handgun at his feet. His soul was all over the yard, surprised and emphatic like hundreds of invisible exclamation points. We were standing right in it. The smell of gunpowder, the smell of blood was rich and sweet. We began to be sick. We took turns throwing up. Our vomit jetted into the grass, pink-colored, smelling clean.

The Tanners' Doberman came bounding over. He licked the brains. We watched his tongue, pink and thin as a slice of ham. We were all touching. We were standing on each other's feet to stay close. The adults in the rest of Lake Mary flowed out of the houses and came streaming toward us. They yanked Bobby and Cooper out of there. They told us we didn't see anything. They called the ambulance, the police, and Mrs. Tanner to get her Doberman.

The wives of Lake Mary swarmed over to the Tanners' screened-in porch to be a little nearer to the tragedy. Jima and me didn't know where to go. We went back inside the shack. Tit looked strange. Her features were softly stricken, noble and unselfish. She did something strange. She cooked us Sloppy Joes. We didn't think she knew how. The Sloppy Joes were delicious and sloppy and tasted like barbecue. Each time Jima and me brought the dripping buns of meat to our lips, we felt like cannibals. We were eating the pharmacist.

At the piano, Flat's chin began to jut out in a menacing Irish manner the way it did when Christ told her what other people should think. Now, Christ was telling her to go forth and offend others. She shot diagonally out of our shack across the lawns of Lake Mary, wild-eyed, her sense of mission so extreme, it added a tilt to her walk. We were disgraced. No one had ever gotten a good look at Flat close-up before. She had not even combed her hair. Jima and me followed her across the grass to see what would happen. Bobby and Cooper saw us and snuck out of their house. We hid in their landscaped bushes together.

The wives were clustered together on the Tanners' screened-in porch, drinking iced tea, contradicting each other on the subject of suicides. Some said suicides went to hell, others said purgatory. Flat edged across the grass until her lips were on the screen. She began to preach.

"The kingdom of heaven is like unto a certain king," she said. The wives screamed. They hadn't seen her coming up to the screen. "The king made a marriage for his son. And sent forth his servants to call them that were bidden to the wedding." She loaded doom into her voice as she said, "*And they would not come.* Again, he sent forth other servants, saying, Tell them which are bidden, Behold, I have prepared my dinner, my oxen and my fatlings are killed and all things are ready, come unto the marriage. But they *made light* of it and *went their ways*, one to his farm, another to his *merchandise.*"

Mrs. Tanner came to the door. "And who are you?" she asked.

"The Lord, I tell you, has put it on my heart to boldly witness that He died for you," Flat said. "I pray that this does not offend you, but I would rather offend you than disobey Him. It is in love that I beg you to ask Jesus Christ into your heart."

"That's just about enough," Mrs. Tanner said through the screen. "Leave now. Or there are authorities who will be more than happy to forcibly remove you. Whoever you are." From the landscaped bushes, Jima and me turned red with shame. Imagine—Flat expulsed from Lake Mary! She shot across the lawn back to our shack at a tilt.

We stayed where we were. We didn't want to be associated with her. Bobby and Cooper stuck with us. I loved them forever for this. We were all in shock. We didn't know what to do.

Dusk fell. Everywhere we looked, men were in danger. They could not be saved. Out on the lake, we saw Little Duck racing his boat in flashy, extreme, slalom curves. Down at the bait shop, men were standing out at the end of the dock under the stars, drinking themselves into a stupor. Jima and me huddled in the cool darkness, watching Bobby and Cooper play with the upside-down metal washtub in their yard, taking turns stepping up on it, shooting themselves in the mouth with a finger, then flopping over on their backs, dead in the cool grass.

III

Where was her smell? I woke up the next morning and my mother was gone. I felt unstable. Big Duck did too. "Where'd she go, God damn you!" he yelled at Flat. The veins in his forehead popped out. The ligaments that held his jaw to his neck bulged furiously under the skin.

Flat looked at him with war in her colorless eyes, her chin jutting out. Her tone was unapologetically menacing. "Bless them that curse you," she hissed. "Do good to them that hate you and pray for them which despitefully use you and persecute you. That ye may be the children of your Father which is in heaven."

If Duck were a hitting man, he'd have struck her hard on the cheek with the flat of his hand, the kind of blow that would topple her off the piano stool and leave her semiconscious on the floor. But he wasn't a hitting man. That was the one thing he promised himself he'd never be the day he ran away from home. He had told us the story now and then, how his mother would make a small plea for the welfare of the children. *Don't you cross me*, his father would say. She'd try to explain. Wham.

When Big Duck tried to stop him, he got hit. One day, his father hit his mother from behind so hard she bit her tongue and it bled on her dress. She tried to dab off the blood, but it kept spurting out. Big Duck couldn't stomach it. Nine years old and he left home, walking down the road with his thumb out. A Christian couple picked him up and drove him to the Farnsworth revival. They all three took Jesus as their Lord and Personal Savior. It lasted until Big Duck met Tit.

"She went to Des Moines, didn't she," Big Duck yelled. "Is she workin' the Fair?" Flat was mum. "She is, isn't she." Big Duck grabbed Jima and me by our shirts and stuffed us into the backseat of the blue roadster. Flat ran fast as a man out of the shack. We didn't know she could run. Big Duck locked the car doors. Flat climbed up on the hood of the roadster and flattened herself against the windshield. "And ye will be hated of all men for my name's sake," Flat hissed through the glass at Duck. "For I am come to set a man at variance against his father, and the daughter against her mother and the daughter-in-law against her mother-in-law. And a man's foes shall be they of his own household." Flat would never allow Big Duck to think his bad behavior was his own idea. Jesus had already allowed for Big Duck's heresies and betrayals. Big Duck was merely fulfilling God's will.

Big Duck got out. He couldn't drive anywhere with a woman on the windshield. He stood in the dirt and smoked a Lucky. Flat sat on the hood, in case he tried to pull a fast one. Jima's gray eyes were speckled with shame. She needed a drink.

Later Big Duck tried again. We were sitting under the tree. Flat was praying inside. Silently, he motioned us into the backseat. He started the engine. We went bumping softly over the railroad tracks, then we went speeding down Highway 69. We were going to Des Moines, to the Iowa State Fair.

Des Moines looked nothing like the cities on television. It was low and gray, with neat, square buildings. It smelled like a cigar. We passed through the downtown and drove out into the countryside again. We turned up a dirt road. On either side, stretching all the way to the horizon, were gently sloping, new-mown hay fields where thousands and thousands of cars were parked. Big Duck grabbed us by the hands and strode across the stubble, yanking us forward faster than we could go. We stumbled along the best we could.

Everywhere we looked, Iowans were letting loose, allow-ing themselves a bit of fun, a little whimsy, some self-display. Farmers we expected to see in manure-encrusted overalls were parading with the missus past the pavilions, both of them wearing huge new jeans and matching white straw cowboy hats. Their red plaid Western-style shirts were brand-new and they matched too, the yokes sculpted to a point in back, the snaps covered with pearl. Under her arm, the missus carried a glitter-dusted ceramic pig the size of a cat. She'd won it on the midway, shooting wooden ducks. The farmer held a feathered Kewpie doll half-naked atop a bamboo stick. They stopped to share a cloud of fluffy pink cotton candy. They were glorious. That slight look of superiority on their faces was justified. They were proud of Iowa, forgetting pride was a sin.

Big Duck pulled us past the sheep barn. In every pen there was a perfectly groomed, perfectly clean sheep or lamb, combed and brushed, petted and named. We passed the horse barn—there were hundreds of stalls. The horses were gleam-ing, their manes braided, their tails tidily trimmed like the tail on a toy. The cattle barn had a thousand stalls. The cows slowly swished their tails back and forth. The bulls snorted. There was so much clean hay on the floor, it didn't smell like a farm—it smelled like a feed store.

We passed the Varied Industry building. We would never see the butter cow. It was all they talked about on the radio. It was life-sized, sculpted of Iowa butter, standing there in a refrigerated glass case. Everyone on the radio said it was so real, you could see the veins in the udder. On a vast lawn there were dozens of spotless John Deere tractors, shiny with yellow and green enamel right from the factory, too clean to ever be used.

Big Duck pulled us into the midst of the swirling, stumbling, mindless crowd of the midway, the sinister district, roped off from the rest with great, looping strings of beckoning colored lights forty feet in the air. Here were the wildly painted rides and naughty amusements, the stomach-churning Ferris wheel pumping its scratchy, worn-out swing music, the breath-smashing Tilt-A-Whirl, loud and rank with rock and roll. Big Duck yanked us into a crowd that surrounded a stage, the girly show. Here he stopped.

The barker was an aging, pimple-faced pervert who leaned lewdly over the podium, spewing spicy descriptions of lovely ladies who, inside the blue tent, for the price of a dollar, you could see naked. His spit hit the microphone in such volume you felt like the sound that came out would infect you with a venereal disease. He introduced two cheap young tramps, one in green satin, one in blue, giving them fancy names, Sissy DuClare all the way from Tulsa, Oklahoma, and Diva Diamondhead from New Orleans. They looked bored and soiled in the bright Iowa sunshine. They chewed gum.

"Last," he said, "but by no means least. And when you see her, you'll agree. From the great dance halls and pleasure palaces of St. Louis, Mizzurrah. Let me introduce you to. The grande dame of the striptease. The gal who put the fanny in fan dance. The bounteous. The unbashful. The bee-*you*-tee-full. Miss Ruby."

Here came my mother, showing off for strangers, slinking out between the curtains in a red satin gown with nothing on underneath. Big Duck grasped me roughly under the arms and hoisted me up in the air. I felt like a fool. "You harlot, you jezebel, come home to your children!" he yelled. His voice was loud and anguished. Men winced when they looked over at ugly me. They didn't want strippers to be family people. Big Duck put me down. He kept it up. "Come home, Letitia, come home," he cried. The men were horrified. They didn't want strippers to have real names.

Two huge bouncers materialized from nowhere. Big Duck pulled out his gun. He fired straight up into the air, ruining Tit's chance to gather a crowd. Everyone scattered. The bouncers got Big Duck in a choke hold. His hat fell to the ground. The state police arrived on foot, running with their guns drawn. Everyone got out of their way. I was caught in a swirling, downward swarm of knees and shoes. My face hit the dirt. I could see Big Duck being dragged away, the heels of his two shoes side by side gouging furrows in the dust. Someone trampled his hat. I felt sick on his behalf. His hat!

When there was space again, I stood up. My too-big jeans with their heavy cuffs were covered with dirt. My sister was nowhere in sight. There were signs I couldn't read over every booth. I didn't know what to do. Behind a counter, the Guess-

Your-Weight man smiled at me, trying to place me. He hesitated to move out from behind his booth, as if he liked to save energy by remaining inert as long as possible. He was an elderly fellow in a plaid vest with popping gold buttons. He wore a white straw boater set way back on his head, so you could see the yellow around the inside rim where he had sweat into it for ten or twelve years. He knew who I was. "Your mother's looking for you," he said. *Your mother's looking for you.* It had a nice ring to it. "You can't find her, can you?" he said.

"No."

He lifted up the hinged counter, squeezed through it, and hooked the velvet rope in the ring, closing his booth. He waddled my way. "Here," he said. "I'll take you to her." He offered me his hand. We walked through the food stands to the freaks. Here were more new smells, more new signs, great, wild letters spelling things out in bright clashing colors of peeling paint. We walked past a man made of wood, a two-headed boy, and a bearded woman. He held open a camouflage-colored curtain and we tiptoed into the private side of the Snake Girl's booth.

Everything was painted green like a jungle. The Snake Girl had a customer walking up the ramp in front. The Weight Man and I stood in silence in the darkness, watching her work. She was a pretty Mexican girl of nineteen or twenty. She stood on a little stool and poked her head up through a hole in her ceiling, which became the floor of the public side. Her hair was long, thick, smooth, and black. Her face was covered with green makeup; a silver cloth nose was pasted over her own. She had dyed her tongue completely red except for a black triangle at the tip. When she darted it in and out, it looked forked. She moved her head sinuously, making noises she construed to be half girl, half snake. It was the glossolalia trick, lots of vowels, a piercing whine and diphthongs, only she added hissing. "Ooo-lai-sssssssss, ah-kaee-sssssssssss," she said with lowered lids. "Aaee-iiee-urrr-sssssssssss." She did this for one minute for two cents.

"She used to eat pebbles and insects," the Weight Man whispered to me. "But no one appreciated it." Below the plywood jungle set, where the customers couldn't see her, she wore regular clothes, Levi's and a red shirt. When the minute was up, she withdrew her head, slinking out of the customer's sight.

"Here she is, Chickie," the Weight Man said. "She was wandering around the burlesque tent."

"No, no." The Snake Girl wrinkled her nose at me. "*She's* got scars. *Mine's* cute." She was only being descriptive. I turned my back on her and pressed my face into the Weight Man's leg. The Snake Girl dropped to her knees in the sawdust to apologize. "No, no, sweetheart, I didn't mean it that way," she said. Too late.

"She didn't," the Weight Man said to me. "Really." The Snake Girl tried to turn my shoulders around to make me forgive her and hug her, but I had a death grip on the Weight Man's thigh. She blubbered a heartfelt Spanish apology. "Chickie," the Weight Man said, nodding his chin toward the ramp. "A customer." Chickie wiped her eyes and climbed up on the stool. She poked her head through the hole in the jungle floor. Above the plywood, she strained and craned her neck, darting her tongue, hissing and speaking snake talk. Below the plywood, she waved good-bye to us with the four fingers of her right hand.

On our way back to his booth, the Weight Man stopped at the cotton candy wagon. "Ever had it?" the Weight Man said to me. I shook my head no. "Give her one," he said to the cotton candy girl. To be handed a fanciful cone of nearly insubstantial, whipped, spun, pink-dyed sugar, to open one's mouth and place a hot tongue on a cloud of pink sweetness, only to have it burst into almost nothing—this was so entrancing and unforgettable that while it lasted, I forgot the existence of everyone I loved and supposedly missed.

I was sitting on the counter of the Weight Man's booth, holding the pink teddy bear he let me choose from his prize shelf, getting the hang of how he guessed weight. He cheated. His foot pushed a pedal that added to the weight of a person as they stood on the scale. They were all too embarrassed at the big number to question him.

There was a lull in the crowd. Coming our way was my sister, her filthy jeans nearly falling off her hips. The sight of her dirty brown hair half out of the clasp, her slanted gray eyes dark with panic, scanning every face in the crowd for me, made my spine feel alert with success. We could get lost among twelve thousand strangers and still find each other. She was leading someone by the hand, someone who could care less. He was a youth with an anchor tattoo on his left forearm and a silver tooth that looked like a steel Chiclet. His face had a cloying hollowness, as if he were poised to be useless. I slid down the counter and stood close to Jima.

"How are things today, Guy?" the Weight Man said to the youth.

"Could be better," Guy said. He said it like everyone owed him a little something. He paused, taking a break. "Let's go, Crane," he said to me.

"You two know each other?" the Weight Man said.

"She's Ruby's," Guy said.

"Ruby's." The Weight Man looked at me, seeing no resemblance. "No kidding."

We followed Guy through the midway to the burlesque tent. Everyone knew him. They all kidded him for ending up with a little responsibility in the form of two children. He stopped everywhere to let them have their fun. It made Jima and me think we now belonged to him. We walked behind the burlesque tent to Guy's trailer. There, standing on the front steps in her red robe, was my mother. She looked at Jima and me like we were two problems. Guy started to lift us into the back of his filthy pickup truck. We didn't want to go.

"Get in the truck," Tit said. As a personal favor to her, she told us, Guy was driving us home. She told us to sit on the produce crates and be still—not to move at all once he started the truck. It wasn't produce in the crates. It was liquor. Tit's vocabulary was always suspect. Guy got behind the wheel. He cranked up the engine. He put the truck in gear. We couldn't believe it. Tit was actually going to stay right there on the front steps of Guy's trailer and wave good-bye to us. It happened too fast for me to dwell on her smell.

The hot night air tore at our hair at sixty miles an hour. We watched the lights of the capital city grow tinier and dimmer. In the darkness on either side of the road, Jima and me could feel the rows of corn snapping open and shut. Our lives had turned blank and sinister. Somewhere along the way, I'd lost my bear. This is what happened to people like us.

—

The piano went unplayed. Flat stayed in the back room, reciting Revelation in a scratchy monotone like a stuck phonograph needle. "And there appeared a great wonder in heaven; a woman clothed with the sun, and the moon under her feet, and upon her head a crown of twelve stars; And she being with child cried, travailing in birth, and pained to be delivered."

Imagine our surprise when there was a knock on our door. No one had ever knocked on our door except the farmer. Flat skittered under the cot to hide. We opened the door. What we saw was a large-boned, stocky-legged, insecure woman shaped like a pear, wearing homemade clothes in terrible colors. Her skirt was vast and lumpy, sewn of olive green cotton. We had seen enough television by then to know that American women did not wear skin-colored, knee-high nylons with the knees exposed above, especially not with scuffed-up, sturdy black walking shoes.

—

The blouse she wore was pale yellow with a not-very-round Peter Pan collar. Her jacket was sewn with no collar, no lapels. The fabric was muslin imprinted with illustrations of edible mushrooms, labeled by their Latin names in calligraphy. On the jacket were too many pins: a spider, a four-leaf clover, a flag we were about to find out was the flag of Switzerland. Her hair was un-American, thick and kinky and pale gray-brown, pulled back on the sides with large plastic barrettes, beyond which it burst out in a frothy cloud that had an unkempt, insectlike effect.

We were gaping, trying to make socioeconomic sense of the woman from *The Children's Book of Knowledge*—because that's what she was. She was trying to make socioeconomic sense of us. The woman consulted her referral card. Jima had signed up for a free in-home demonstration at the Iowa State Fair. The woman cleared her throat and asked if Jima was Jima Cavanaugh.

"Yes, ma'am," Jima said.

"Is this the family?" she asked.

"Yes, ma'am," Jima said.

We were all pretending. The woman was pretending she was a high-pressure door-to-door salesman. We were pretending we had $99.99 to spend on books. The woman scrapped her step-by-step sales pitch. Her eyes grew maternal. "Nice family," she said.

"Say thank you," Jima said.

"Thank you," I said.

"You're well-come." The way the woman said it we could hear the two separate words that conveyed the original meaning. She paused. She was looking at the two of us, wondering if it was very right or very wrong to sell girls like us encyclopedias.

She did something spontaneous next. She sat, landing with a bit of a thud in the dirt on her side of the door, folding her big legs beneath her to the extent possible. She opened up the scary brown satchel and pulled out a volume. "Does this interest you?" she said and held the pages wide open, facing us, showing us beautiful, colorful flags from the nations of the world. Jima sat down too. I squatted, lowering my head close to the page so I could see. "Can you point to the flag of Switzerland that matches my pin?" she said. I did.

She told us Switzerland was a tiny neutral country in Europe, known for chocolate, clocks, and the Alps. She was born there. One day, she hoped to go back.

On the page filled with photographs of dogs, she asked us to point to our favorite kind. I liked Lassie. Jima liked the Great Pyrenees with the brandy cask beneath its chin. The woman asked us if there was anything we wanted to know a little more about.

"What's in there on sex?" I said.

"Plenty." The woman turned to the special section on the systems of the human body. A man's naked body was illustrated in color with seven plastic overlays showing each of his amazing systems. She showed us the reproductive system overlay. There was a mistake, but I didn't mention it. The man's dick was not erect. She showed us the endocrine system with its green hypothalamus, its yellow thyroid, its tiny purple pituitary. She showed us the circulatory system with red blood leaving the heart, blue returning. She showed us the digestive system with miles and miles of large intestine to refine our waste.

"How much?" Jima said. Flat was under the cot where we kept our night-crawler money.

The woman blinked. Her voice got softer and sweeter. She was shy. We loved her for being so gentle and un-American. "It's quite a bit," she said. Her voice dropped down to a whisper. "You pay by the month, a little bit every month for quite a while. You can buy my demonstration set for less." She tried to say the number, but she lost her voice.

"How much do you have?" she finally said.

Jima slipped into the back room. I followed her. Flat was holding our jar of quarters to her chest with both arms as if it were hers. "And there appeared another wonder in heaven, and behold a great red dragon," Flat said, her voice weak and staticky. Jima wrested the jar out of Flat's grasp. I was impressed.

"What was that noise?" the woman asked Jima when Jima handed her the jar.

Jima looked her dead in the eye and said, "The radio."

"Having seven heads and ten horns, and seven crowns upon his heads," Flat said. "And his tail drew the third part of the stars of heaven."

The woman counted our quarters. Twelve dollars and fifty cents. "That will do," she said. She went out to the car. Huffing and puffing, she returned with a new box containing the full set, all twenty-six volumes, bound in red leather and embossed with gold. This was no demonstration set. This set was brand-new. The smell of the ink almost made me keel over.

"Thank you," we said, grateful that she got back in her station wagon and drove away before Flat got to the part about fornication.

Jima and me pored over the illustrations, extracting what information we could. One thing was for sure: *A* was for Ant.

Black ants had taken over the pharmacist's yard. I watched them come filing out of the anthill by the hundreds. Now the illustration showed me what was inside the hill—an underground city like Des Moines with streets and tunnels leading to food storage rooms. A long line of ants was shown carrying leaves from the woods back to the nest to store. I had never seen so much food in my life. Other smaller rooms were used as nurseries where baby ants bundled in white were cared for by nurse ants. Deepest and darkest of all was the vast underground chamber where the huge queen ant sequestered herself to lay egg after tiny egg.

A drawing of the ant's brain made it look huge. The ingenuity of their jaws was emphasized. Ants used their jaws to carry awkward loads hundreds of times their weight and size. They were shown using their jaws like spades to dig new nests in the dirt, like saws to sever twigs, like machetes to kill. Ants waged war. One picture showed thousands of red ants marching into battle against brown ants. Their front lines clashed as red and brown soldiers rose up on their rear legs, one-on-one, to wrestle, maim, and stab each other to death. Brave enough to defend the colony, organized enough to feed everyone—apparently, ants were smarter than we were. An ant never sat there wondering to itself, *What will become of me?*

—

It was Indian summer. The afternoon sun was yellow and calm on my arms. The wind had lost its persistent, bracing tug. It was down to a wisp again, a breeze. The locusts were humming their plaintive, subliminal chord. The fenced fields of harvested corn stretched to the horizon. The pale champagne-colored stubble was beautiful in its own way, the vertical stalks were blunt, broken at the base like blond pencil marks against the dark background of the soil.

We heard it at the bait shop. For the third year in a row, Iowa farmers had produced a record harvest. Now there was too much corn on the market. It drove the price down below where it was when there wasn't enough.

Little Duck was staying in town half the time. Flat was staying under the cot. Our lives felt up for grabs. We opened our encyclopedias for reassurance, looking at the pictures of the wonderful world out there.

There was a disturbance in the air, an inaudible assault that hammered away at the ease and warmth of the afternoon sun.

It ate away at our enthrallment with the illustrations in *The Children's Book of Knowledge*. We kept looking out the window, Jima and me, as if something wrong were coming our way. The pitch of the imminent thing grew terrible, ruining the emotional equilibrium supplied by the perfection of our twenty-six volumes, *A* to *Z*.

A vehicle pulled up to our shack, a dark green van bearing a gold insignia. Flat stayed under the cot. Jima opened the door. It wasn't the people from *The Children's Book of Knowledge* this time. It was the county. They snatched us up and locked us in the van. Our shack was condemned. They were already roping it off with Flat still inside as we rode away. Someone had finally turned us in.

—

I had never lived in architecture before. The convent was half church, half castle. There were arches that led to arches. There were loggias that led to loggias. There were chapels that led to chapels. And there were crucifixes everywhere. A county worker walked me up the front steps and handed me off to Sister Peg. Jima was too old for convent life. The county was calling around the state, trying to find a bed for her in a home for troubled girls. Sister Peg took my hand. One of my lice jumped up onto her habit. She screamed. Into the bathtub I went. My introduction to convent life was to be harshly, repeatedly scrubbed everywhere.

There were two kinds of nuns, I would quickly learn. With the best kind, you could easily separate the face and mood of the woman from the habit. With the worst, the face was indistinguishable from the habit. Sister Peg was the worst. Over and over, she washed me *there*. To cover up what she'd done, Sister Peg dressed me in an overlarge maroon Catholic school jumper. A gold crucifix was clasped around my neck. Sister Peg brushed my hair straight back into a punishing, humorless ponytail, which drew attention to the exposed white deformity of my forehead. Bingo—I looked married to Christ. Ten years old and I was about to become a nun.

I shared a room on the second floor with the cleaning woman. Mrs. Sodstrum had round black eyes with long, thick lashes. Her face was round and pale brown. Beneath her soft broken nose were peacefully smiling lips. She wore her blue-black hair in a braid that fell to her waist. She had been a beautiful Hawaiian girl before she became a widow. Every day she wore a green uniform with a round, white collar to clean the long, quiet floors of the convent halls with her bucket and her string mop, dunking, sloshing, slapping, swishing, washing the marble with the same strokes in the same sequence, humming sweetly, taking neat backward steps with her lovely, large, light brown bare feet. The songs she hummed were island songs. Sometimes she sang the words. They were all vowels. "A-i-ai He-e-i-a la e-ka na-lu e he-e a-na e-a e-a e-a e-a," she sang, her voice echoing a little against the marble. There was a gentle suction sound each time she lifted the soles and heels of her feet from the marble. My job was to move the bucket along for her and, when she lowered the mop between the double rubber rollers, to crank the lever that squeezed them shut, removing the excess water. Afterward, we washed out the mop and stored it in the utility closet, handle down. We rested in our room.

Our room was sweet with white walls and neat twin beds. By the door was a framed illustration of Jesus on the cross. I couldn't read, but I knew what the caption said: *Father, forgive them for they know not what they do.* Our window overlooked the convent's formal garden. A stone path led up to a statue of the Blessed Virgin. There was snow on the ground around her now. Someone had shoveled the path that led up to the Virgin but left the cap of snow on her head. Mrs. Sodstrum told me beautiful bulbs of all colors would burst forth in bloom out there at Easter time. The sputtering steam from our radiator made me feel cozy and warm.

—

For my educational testing, Sister Peg sent me to Sister Anne, the best kind of nun—her face was her own, and she kept her hands to herself. Brisk, clear, well-executed charity—there was no better kind, if charity was your fate. Sister Anne's eyes were pale blue, authoritative, and steady. Her skin was the bluish white of English royalty, with flushed, rosy cheeks that came not from makeup, but from walking briskly one hour daily, rain or shine. From the television dramas I'd seen in the bait shack, I could easily envision Sister Anne as a real woman not married to Christ, wearing cable-knit sweaters and straight wool skirts. Her neck scarves would be saucy and tied so tight, the corners would stay pointy and alluring all day. Her brown hair would fall across one side of her face. She would write newspaper articles that saved whole countries from tyranny and persecution.

"Crane," she said, kneeling down, looking me in the eye, taking me by the shoulders with respect for my body in a way that made me wonder how I'd gotten by without it all these years, "I will do right by you. You will be happy." It was her job to prepare me to attend the Catholic school across the court-yard. Girls were educated in the north half of the school, boys in the south. First, Sister Anne administered placement tests. That went quickly. I could neither add nor read. She sat me down with her first-grade primer to teach me to read. The letters were wavy and blurry. I couldn't see.

"I am outraged," Sister Anne said. "No one along the way has figured out that you need eyeglasses." We bundled up and walked down Main Street to the nun's optometrist. The frames I had my heart set on were expensive—black horn-rims like the ones worn by scientists on TV, moving about in their white lab coats, pouring one test tube of dry ice into another. Sister Anne dipped into the pocket in her habit for the extra expense.

Now I could effortlessly recognize the pictures of things that began with the five letters most commonly used in English. I rattled them off for Sister Anne: *C*at, *O*wl, *S*nake, *A*pple, *T*urtle. I read my first sentence: "Cat sat." Finally, the code that revealed the fruits of Western civilization!

—

Three times a day, we had convent food. It was like nothing I'd seen in *Life*. It was cooked in huge steel pots and pans and ladled onto our plates in a stingy gesture that left most of the food still in the spoon. It was either brown, white, or gray. Once in a while, our food was red, and all the nuns were happier.

Morning and evening, the bells in the convent tolled out some dour, off-key dirge. My spirits plummeted. *Then sings my soul, My Savior God, to Thee.* I missed my sister and the smell of her dirty brown hair. *You made* (dum-dum). *Me cry* (dum-dum). I missed Little Duck. I told Sister Anne I'd had a sister and a brother. "That's nice, dear," she said, humoring me. The county records had not mentioned siblings. Sister Anne assumed I was nurturing a typical orphan fantasy. "You can talk to them at night when you say your prayers to Jesus."

—

Across the hall from the room I shared with Mrs. Sodstrum was the bathroom for all the nuns. I panicked when I walked in there. My footsteps echoed on the cold, white tile. The unnatural, nasal-piercing sting of bleach filled the air. There were multiple stalls. I could hear the nuns tinkling. They frowned as they scrubbed their hands, as if their hands did wrong things when they weren't looking. Some grunted and groaned forever in the stalls, stinking up the place mightily with their daily accomplishment. Where was mine? I hadn't shit since the county took me away. I mentioned this to Sister Anne.

"Have an Ex-Lax," she said, offering me a tablet. I assumed an Ex-Lax would make me shit Xs. I swallowed it. "Give it an hour," she said.

What an experience. Long after it was over, I would dream about it, always the same dream of primal humiliation. I would be sitting in the chapel, bowing my head in prayer, when my anatomy suddenly, arbitrarily became a shit gun, ejecting a round of so-called ammunition in a messy, pressurized blast. No one was spared.

My stomach settled down. I got the hang of indoor plumbing. I began to enjoy the cold, clean feel of the porcelain toilet, the loud, frightening roar of water released on demand when I pushed the flush lever. From the window, I could see where that water came from. It was stored in a silver water tower, a sideways egg on stilts in the middle of the town green. In painted black capital letters, it said ARNOLD to people riding by on Route 69. I would review my accomplishment. There was a lot of *Na*, some *Ca*, an occasional *I*. Perhaps I was shitting Hawaiian. I'd push the lever. Wham-o. What I'd made went churning into some underground public tank along with everyone else's.

—

Mrs. Sodstrum had a fondness for green apples. She kept a bowlful of Granny Smiths in the window of our room. At the end of our workday, we each ate one. First, she turned back into herself. She took out her braid. Her hair sprung out, holding the tight blue-black curves of the braid. She put on a sarong. She would sit on her little woven rattan mat with both legs folded gracefully to one side. I sat the same way on my woven mat. We ate our Granny Smiths. When I told Mrs. Sodstrum I had siblings, she believed me. She asked what they were like. Jima, I said, was a drunk, Little Duck, a sex fiend. She was pleased. She was too, she said. Most Hawaiians were, she said. On her dresser she kept a gold-framed photograph of her eighteen-year-old son in Waikiki. She showed his white face to me, confessing a dramatic underage romance with his father, an ensign in the U.S. Navy.

We listened to Hawaiian music. She would prop up the cardboard album cover against the bureau so we both could see it. She would jiggle the LP down over the spindle of the record player and lower the needle. Twaaaang. The guitar was drunk. It oozed up chords and down again, wobbling every step of the way. It was the exact sound you'd expect from the world pictured on the album cover, a world of orchids, monkeys, parrots, palm trees, pineapples, and sunsets. Once in a while, if she knew the translation, she'd speak the American words to me beneath the Hawaiian melody, her round black eyes darkening and brightening at the same time to express passion, her heart happy and peaceful with memories of whole evenings of physical love.

"*Wailana*," she said, "means 'Drowsy Waters.' *Ke-a-lo-ha e ma-liv ma i o e*: Like drowsy waters are thy deep-lit eyes, love. *O-i-a-i-ke-a lo - ha i ke ki no*: And my heart the flower thirsting deep on hope's brink. Oh give me to drink thy tender sighs, love," she translated. "Give me to drink again, give me to drink. The scent of your hair is here at my heart, love. Old kisses burn softly along my veins, love. But oh, where are you and why are we apart, love. Without you naught of joy remains." I was mesmerized.

One afternoon, when one of her favorite instrumentals began to play, Mrs. Sodstrum jumped up and did the hula. She placed her arms parallel straight out in front, hands together, palms facing out toward me. She swayed her hips from side to side, not to show off, but with a gently rolling motion like Marilyn Monroe on television when she did it to please herself more than you. Mrs. Sodstrum broke out into a side step, her hips wiggling ably, her arms waving gracefully to the side.

I wanted to learn. Because Mrs. Sodstrum was born a pagan, Sister Anne had to clear this practice with Mother Superior. Permission was granted. We did the love hula for the men we loved. I loved Cooper Tanner.

—

I flew through my reading lessons, covering five years of instruction in five months. I read straight through Sister Anne's encyclopedia. Those half-naked men in a sunny seaside setting with a temple lined with columns in the *G* volume of *The Children's Book of Knowledge* were Greeks. *G* was also for Germany—the place where rosy-cheeked blonde girls wore embroidered skirts to dance in front of a castle in snow-topped mountains. Those layers of dinosaur skulls and snails and shells beneath the surface of the earth's crust were Geology.

E, I learned, was for Egypt, the home of the River Nile, a valley so fertile that the Egyptians could easily grow sufficient crops to feed themselves, and, because of this, they had time to turn their attention to other things. They invented the art of writing and the science of weaving. They learned to build temples in the desert that were astronomically sophisticated and accurate even by our standards today, the greatest of which was the Great Pyramid. In the photograph, to show the scale of the Great Pyramid, there was a tiny robed man riding a tiny camel across the sand in front of it. If Jima could read, she could have made a Great Pyramid out of sand as the center-piece of the Land of Ablah-Dablah.

What had our three parents been so afraid of? The forty-four experts who wrote and reviewed the content of the encyclopedia never mentioned Satan. They worked together to create a cohesive, uniform, cheerful view of the world, a view that encouraged a healthy curiosity, a decent amount of civic pride, and a gentle love of people and their ways.

F was not only for flower and fur, but for someone important who looked just like me, except that her hair was longer. When I asked Sister Anne her name, she said, "Benjamin Franklin."

To catch me up in math, Sister Anne gave me a set of beautiful blocks in precisely graduated lengths and coded colors. I learned addition, subtraction, multiplication, and division without knowing it. I made my own games with the blocks. Now and then, Sister Anne would look at some equation I'd made. "That's advanced," she would say, more to herself than to me.

—

In the fall, we were ready. Sister Anne took me by the hand and led me personally across the courtyard to the girls' side of the Catholic school. I entered the sixth grade.

My repulsive appearance made me the exciting new butt of Tyrene's jokes. Tyrene was a tall, sneaky girl with rashes and an overbite. She pulled my chair out from under me when I went to sit down. I plummeted to the floor, hitting the back of my head on the chair seat. She slapped a KICK ME sign on my back—and everyone did. When I figured out how to never turn my back on Tyrene, she and her gang met me after school. They held me down while she punched and kicked—always in the torso, never in the face, or the nuns would know. "Don't tell, or you'll get really hurt," she said. As soon as Tyrene was done, I brushed the dirt off my uniform skirt and went charging back across the courtyard to help my friend and roommate wash the convent floors.

I was getting better at the hula. Mrs. Sodstrum opened her straw trunk and brought out a raffia skirt for me. She let me choose my own paper-flower jewelry from dozens of bright red, orange, and hot pink bracelets, anklets, leis, and crowns— all handmade of crepe paper by herself in younger days. We dressed ourselves to the hilt. She even put lipstick and rouge on me. She taught me the hop, which was done in a crouching position. No matter how low she crouched, she could still hop, her arms always graceful and level, her hands never ceasing to gently wave. She was limber for being so round. To finish, she hopped around in a circle, then jumped up with a Hawaiian whoop and sent her hips gyrating wildly. She was magnificent. There was so much more I had to learn.

—

Corporal punishment by day, crucifixes by night. And sometimes, in between, the hula. There was something about my new life—all I could think about was sex. On the cross, Jesus himself set the tone, so young, so bloody, so passive, and so very naked, his mouth going slack, his irises just starting to roll up into his head in a capitulation uncannily similar to sexual climax. At night, my dreams were filthy. I dreamed I was back in our shack. Tyrene's goons would be holding me down as usual while Tyrene beat me up, but then, of all people, it was Jump who would rescue me, yanking me out of the fray by my Catholic ponytail, caveman style, then throwing me over his shoulder to carry me out to the reeds. He'd picked up a tip or two from Sister Peg, soaping me over and over *there*.

—

Ants lived together in harmony, I read in Sister Anne's *Encyclopedia Britannica. All for one and one for all*—that would be their motto if ants had mottoes. Ants cared for their young, ministered to the sick, and waited hand and foot on the queen. Ants were industrious. They persevered. They could communicate in code with their antennae. No task they undertook was too difficult for them to conquer. They were tidy and clean. They disposed of their refuse. They defended the colony from intruders. The ingenuity and thoroughness of ants when it came to the provision of food was legendary. Some ants milked lice for honeydew the way farmers milked cows for milk. Ants herded the lice from corn plant to corn plant so the lice could suck the honeydew from the leaves. Leaf-cutter ants traveled in pairs in long lines to collect leaves, which they carried back to the nest. Honeypot ants bloated their bellies with honey, then climbed down into the food storage room deep underground in the nest and hung upside down from the ceiling like living honey jars, waiting to feed members of the colony mouth-to-mouth during the long cold winter.

There were twenty thousand different kinds of ants in the world. Partnerships between ants and the plants they lived in were well documented. The plants provided the ants with food and shelter; the ants defended the plants from predatory insects and mammals. One species of ant, however, had everyone worried—the fire ant. The fire ant had come to North America from South America on ships, in people's boxes and trunks. It was slowly destroying the native ant population in the southeastern United States. Fire ants won every war. They could survive a flood. They were immune to disease. They could turn carnivore.

I took a closer look at the little yellowish red things in the courtyard. "They're just ants," Sister Maureen, the science teacher said when I asked her what kind they were. I watched them discover a dead caterpillar. Within minutes, a line formed, flowing across the pavement along a jerky, eerily unvarying path. Each ant collected a piece of the caterpillar and carried it back to the colony. The return journey did not duplicate the outgoing one, though its pattern included similar elements, arbitrary angles, transversing some obstacles, circumventing others. After the caterpillar was dismembered and removed to the food storage room inside the nest, there was a pause in activity. A scout discovered a Three Musketeers wrapper streaked with small melted bits of chocolate and stray nougat. Word went out. A line of ants converged on the wrapper.

I played God. I moved their food. I only moved it three feet, but the first ant to encounter the change was taken aback. Her feelers madly swept the vicinity as she rocked in place, seeking a clue. Her hesitation caused a pileup in the line. There must have been complaints from the rear. She wasn't yet convinced of what direction to take, but she obliged, venturing blindly forth, zigging and zagging, until—Bingo!—she found it. And every ant behind her in line unnecessarily followed the same jazzy little route, feelers sweeping madly, blundering up to the now-phantom food source, then zigging and zagging forward to the real one. All these ants were female. Male ants were only needed once a year. They flew up to the queen, mated, then died.

One day I saved my green apple to feed them. I took a bite out of it to get it started. They were thrilled. Word went out. They found it and swarmed over it until my apple looked as if it were made of ants. Across the courtyard, a competing colony cracked the food alert code. Hundreds of them came marching forward to challenge these ants to the rights to my apple. A vast turf battle began. I had started a war. The incumbents took on the invaders in hand-to-hand combat, rearing up on their legs and waving their feelers, dodging around each other until one got the other in a wrestling hold. Some pairs were evenly matched and stayed locked in combat for hours. Others got off a quick bite, a decisive sting, or chopped the opponent in two. The victor then carried the deceased in pieces back to the nest to store as food.

It looked to me as if all the ants in the world were right here, but both sides sent for fresh recruits. Hundreds more ants advanced from each side, marching along their special jerky unvarying paths to join in combat. One large, strong soldier removed her slain comrade from the fray in one piece. To carry the corpse back to the nest, the soldier clamped the dead ant's head in her jaws so the body was sticking out lengthwise in front. Imagine a human soldier marching energetically off the battlefield with a dead comrade sticking straight out of his jaws. And not only on level ground. As if she lived in a world without gravity, this soldier marched straight up the vertical side of a wooden crate with the body in her jaws, never missing a step.

The war over the apple went on until a small, precocious squadron of special incumbent forces found its way back to the invaders' nest and killed the queen. All soldiering was done. The invading workers went to work for the incumbents. Harmony reigned once more.

—

I was ugly enough to become a nun, but I was lacking an essential docility when it came to science. Sister Maureen taught geology straight from the Bible. Her lesson on creation began with her reading from the book of Genesis: God had made the world in seven days. I'd watched a man make a lake. It took ninety days—with earthmoving equipment. How much longer would it take God to make an entire rotating planet with lakes and rivers, mountains and forests, canyons and mesas, oceans and islands, jungles and ice caps, Germany and Greece—not to mention Egypt—when all he had available were gasses and dust? I could not play along.

"How old is the earth?" Sister Maureen asked the class. She meant for us to calculate this by counting backward through the begats in Genesis, adding up the years lived by each patriarch. The sum total she was looking for was around three thousand five hundred years. No one raised a hand. "You," she said, pointing at me with an air of challenge, testing me to see if I had yet learned to bend my will to the will of God.

"Oh, around forty-five hundred million years," I said, reciting one of the many facts I cherished from Sister Anne's encyclopedias, my voice calm, my eyes defiant like Tit's used to be when she knew she was right. Carbon samples of the earth's crust dated its formation in that range. Sister Maureen flew at me with her ruler.

"Show me your hands," she commanded. I did. It took about twelve whacks on the back of each hand to draw blood. I refused to cry. Information mattered. As if my bowels were backing me up, I'd only been able to shit *C*s.

Sister Anne was unnerved. I'd skipped a grade in reading and two grades in math—I was now doing advanced algebra. Yet I was getting an F in science. I failed every test. She counseled me. "This is a religious school," she said. "Our curriculum is based on faith in God. Faith in God allows us to accept mysteries beyond the expertise of any science made by man."

"Did God make math?" I asked.

Sister Anne was trapped. If He didn't, we shouldn't be study-ing it. If He did, he made science too. Around and around in circles we went. I could make every line of questioning Sister Anne came up with end in a trap. She prayed over me. She had my IQ tested. It came back too high, so she sent me to be tested again. My score was confirmed. She ceased begrudging me my thirst for information of the provable kind. She discharged me from a future as a celibate holy penitent in a habit. In her determination to find a secular adoptive family for me, she was prepared to do something heretical. She was willing to contact the Methodists.

First I needed a case history. *Crane, parentage unknown.* That was all there was in writing from the county about me. Our three parents weren't in any census. Sister Anne sat down at her desk and uncapped her pen. She wrote a heartbreaking summation, cocking her head to one side, looking off misty-eyed into time, fulfilling my vision of her as a newspaper reporter in a cable-knit sweater, her brown hair falling across one eye, writing articles that saved people from tyranny and persecution. She made me the orphaned daughter of a judge from Adel. My mother had died in childbirth. I was scalded as an infant by a careless nanny, hence the deformed forehead. The nanny also pushed me down the stairs, with the useful result that, regarding my early upbringing, I was afflicted with total amnesia. The only thing in my case history that was true was my IQ. I was a genius.

—

All spring, I could feel Methodists peeping at me. In the cha-pel during Mass, in math class across the courtyard, during my rounds up and down the convent halls with Mrs. Sodstrum,

I could feel their disappointment. What could you do with a repulsive-looking girl? Well, I didn't like them either. Glancing across the pew at them, looking over my shoulder as they slipped out of the classroom, I detected questionable motives hovering around their heads as clear as ink. People who wanted a grown child were missing something, and they intended to make the child supply it.

Almost overnight, I produced a matching pair of tits of considerable size. All the nuns were impressed. They thought I was the flat-chested type. I knew better. Wasn't my mother Letitia Grund? Now I filled out the front of my uniform. Sister Peg could hardly keep her eyes off me. Other things happened that Mrs. Sodstrum explained. She gave me a cowrie-shell love amulet to celebrate my womanhood. I would sometimes hold the album when we listened to Hawaiian love songs and imagine myself to be as beautiful as the woman on the cover. Her lips were half an inch from the lips of her secret island lover. The pointed shadows of the palm leaves flickered on their cheekbones, offering privacy. *Oh give me to drink thy tender sighs, love. Give me to drink again, Give me to drink.*

Suddenly, some Methodists were interested. A couple came back twice. Not having a sex life put Sister Anne at a disadvantage. She couldn't pick up their skeevy vibes. This couple volunteered at the hospital. They owned a three-bedroom home with a swimming pool in the best school district. These were the advantages that Sister Anne saw instead of looking askance at the thudding prurience of these two particular humans. He was fat in a loose rumbly way that told me his glands were dialed down so low that his food formed fluffy tissue instead of muscle. All his fluffiness could be clearly seen rippling obscenely beneath his thin polyester pants and see-through shirt. The softness around his mouth embarrassed me, as if I were looking at something children weren't meant to see.

His wife was the same height and weight as he. Her hair was long, thin, and brownish gray. She wore it pulled across the forehead to one side with a childish green barrette. She passively stared into space at a point about five feet in front of her. He stared at me. While he stared, he reached into his jacket pocket and pulled out a doughnut with pink icing. He ate it in three bites, letting crumbs fall down his front, and all the time that he chewed, he stared.

They told Sister Anne they'd take me. All that remained to be done was the paperwork. Sister Anne had to confirm their annual income and check their personal references. For the next few days, Sister Anne winked triumphantly whenever she passed me in the convent halls. Then the last reference came in bad. Worse than bad. Now she winced when we passed, horrified at what she'd almost done.

—

A lovely, young, barren couple moved to Arnold and joined the Methodist church. The wife had had polio when she was a child. One leg was weak. She couldn't adopt an infant. She wasn't supposed to lift anything heavier than a cast-iron skillet. The Methodists called Sister Anne to book an appointment.

I heard my new mother before she heard me. Her voice preceded her, country-loud, coarse, and candid, volunteering answers that were officially wrong before they were even asked. "If it's all the same to you, Sister," Ollie Hopkins said to Sister Anne as they made their way up the echoing convent hall, "Ray will wait in the car. He don't want no part of no daughter. He's just doing this for me."

Sister Anne was more savvy now. She was suspicious. "Let me clarify," Sister Anne said. "If you're looking for someone to compensate for you in terms of household chores, this girl is not for you. She isn't a workhorse."

"Sister!" Ollie said. "I got a Hoover! It don't take me but an hour—everything's on one floor!" Her enthusiasm somehow put Sister Anne on the defensive.

"I'm only suggesting she's a scholar," Sister Anne said.

"Does she need love?" Ollie said. "Because if it's love you're looking for, Ollie's got more love to give than Christ himself can shake a stick at—no offense. Marriage is lonely, Sister. No one tells you that."

I was sitting in the library, scrubbed, brushed, and hyperventilating in my uniform, eavesdropping while pretending to be engrossed in a book. Ollie came through the doorway. Her hair was dyed peroxide blonde, curled up in a tight flip. Her chin was fat and round, her skin rough and red. She walked with a halting, bovine sway, the result of the polio. Her right leg was weaker and shorter, thin as a broom handle from the knee to the ankle. In her pink oxford-cloth shirtwaist dress, Ollie had not succeeded in evoking her idol, demure and dainty Doris Day, due to her earthiness, her vitality, and, of course, her build. Her breasts were big and her hips were big. In between, her waist was big.

Ollie's eyes grew moist as they landed on me. Her lips lifted in a smile half pleasure, half pride. It was the first time any human had been deluded on the subject of my looks. "Bless her heart," Ollie said. "All she needs is bangs. Bangs and a bob, and

she'll be cute as a button." Ollie lowered her voice to give Sister
Anne a tip. "A ponytail don't do nothing for a gal with a flat
chin, Sister. Makes her look like a nun—no offense. You wait
'til Ollie gets her hands on her. She'll look as good as Ollie."

Sister Anne consulted me silently. *It's in your hands*, her eyes
were saying. We'd worked out a signal. I closed my book. That
meant *yes*.

—

The papers were signed. Sister Anne walked us down the hall
to the door to the outside world. Slowly, gracefully, she dropped
back a step, then two, establishing an interval that implied
separation. I looked back over my shoulder at her. Her eyes
urged me forward, promising me nothing would go wrong. I
heard the slap-slap-slap of bare feet. Mrs. Sodstrum was running toward us bearing a little straw trunk. She asked Sister
Anne's permission to give me a pagan costume. Folded inside
were the raffia skirt, my own orange muumuu, and a full set
of hot pink paper-flower jewelry. Permission was given. Mrs. S.
bowed to me. "*Aloha au la oe*," she said. *I love you.*

I bowed to Mrs. Sodstrum and said it back to her, "*Aloha au
la oe*." All that early training in glossolalia had made it easy to
pick up Hawaiian.

—

Outside, the sun was bright. At the curb in a green Plymouth
was Ollie's husband, Ray. Ray had thin hips and a wide belt.
His blue cotton short-brimmed fishing hat was pierced with
grommet-bound airholes. He wore it pulled down on his forehead just above the eyebrows. His aftershave was new to me. I

soon found out it was called Mennen, which seemed like a good word for a world made only of men. He stared straight ahead as Ollie asked me to climb in front next to him. I kept my eyes on the chrome of the car radio in order to come off as brave as Sister Anne had promised Ollie I was. We left town behind. The intense, fertile blue of the summer sky filled the windshield. Through the open window, I smelled earth, manure, corn. There were careening twists and turns that swayed my body left and right. There were dips and bumps that made my stomach feel queasy. Road dust rose in funnels beneath our wheels, up, up into the air, and sifted slowly down again through the open window onto our skin. Ray slowed down to make a left turn. I smelled my old lake. I smelled my old life. I was back in Lake Mary.

IV

Oooooooooooooooo. I stood in the driveway, close to Ollie, shivering. Our sides were completely touching. I let her lead me up the steps and into my room. Yards and yards of double-ruffled pink organza poured off the curtain rod. The wallpaper was pink stripes, the bedspread pink roses. The bed itself wore a skirt. The lamp on the nightstand had a pink shade. The rug, also pink, was deep shag. I had my own wooden desk, which Ollie had painted pink. The same paint she brushed on the bookcase, though the books themselves were gray. They concerned accounting, auditing, adjusting, appraising, things Ray needed to know when he got his appraiser's license. I walked over to my window and looked out. Lake Mary, still and green, lay in its lovely lake bed. At the far shore, our steadfast tree cast a loose shadow of deep shade over the water. Our shack was gone. There was a white scar on the ground where it used to be. Next door was the pharmacist's empty house. It was deafening, the inaudible roar, the silent, booming, endless, phosphorescent after-hum of his gun. I threw up. It was pink.

—

Ollie made up the rules that were to govern our little family, beginning with the evening meal—we would prepare it together. For our first supper, she picked an easy recipe from the pages of the *Ladies Home Journal* that called for ingredients that were already food. "Drain one can tuna fish," Ollie read. Ollie's main kitchen tool was the electric can opener. She showed me how to jigger the rim of a can of tuna fish between the two blades. She let me push ON. The motor hummed as the top of the little can obediently revolved. A magnet grabbed the jagged lid. The open can dropped to a stop.

Ray sat at the kitchen table, shielding himself from involvement by reading the newspaper, holding it wide open, blocking himself entirely from view. "Don't call Ray *Father*," she said, moving on to rule number two. "This wasn't his idea. He don't want no part of it. If you call him Father, it will remind him of that. No, you just call him Ray."

"Ray," I said, quickly and emphatically.

"Not now," she said. "When it's time to call him something." She read from the page. "Stir in one can Campbell's Cream of Mushroom Soup." We opened can number two. "Me, you can call Ollie. Don't call me *Mother*. Because I ain't your mother and never will be. Everybody's only got one. You can't help it if yours died in childbirth."

Ollie read from the page. "Sprinkle one can of French's Fried Onion Rings over the top." I had the hang of it by now. I opened can number three. "Bake at 375 degrees for forty minutes or until brown." Ollie set the timer.

"You I can call *Daughter*," Ollie said. "See, I can't have children. Dennis, my first husband I married when I was barely seventeen, he kicked my womb in. He's dead now, thank

heaven. Bastard beat me every Friday night. Look at my nose."
Ollie thrust her face in profile against the green wall. "See
them bumps?"

I looked. Now that she mentioned it, the ridge of her nose
looked like knuckles. "Ma'am, I do see them," I said.

"Don't call me *ma'am*."

"*Ollie*."

"Them three bumps are where he broke my nose three different times. There's a man in Chicago can fix this," she said.
"He cuts you open, pushes the pieces of bone back in a row and
glues them tight. Then he sews you up again. I'm going to see
him, soon as Ray can afford it."

Behind his newspaper, Ray snorted.

"Look here, Daughter. Here's what they can't fix," Ollie
said. She inserted the fingers of her left hand into the soft,
important digestive organs between her waist and her crotch.
"I can't tell you how many times I got kicked here. See, first
they sock you in the nose so you fall down, then when you're
down, they kick you. Ruptures the spleen. He got his in the
end. Used to get drunk and walk down the railroad tracks. Got
hit by a train and dragged," Ollie said. She was quiet for a
moment, as if reliving the day and the way the tragic news was
brought to her.

"One more thing, Daughter," Ollie said.

"Yes, Ollie."

"Your name is Princess now."

"Yes, Ollie."

She busied herself for a moment, all the while intending to
surprise me to see if the new name would stick. "Princess!"

"Yes, Ollie." It stuck. She was pleased.

While Crispy Tuna Noodle Bake baked, Ollie confided in me. "I could whip up hash, mash up turnips, or make milk toast," she said. "All that farmer food would be fine with Ray. But Grace Paludy next door already got me pegged for a hog farmer from Mason City. So just in case she busts in here unannounced, I don't cook nothin' but modern."

The timer went off. Crispy Tuna Noodle Bake was ready to eat. Ollie set a trivet on the table. She placed our hot casserole dish on the trivet.

"Ray," Ollie said. Ray finished reading the article, then folded the newspaper in half and put it down. Ollie bowed her head. Here it comes, I thought, waiting for lengthy ravings about my depraved soul. "Bless this food to our use and us to thy service," Ollie said, snapping open her paper napkin on the word *service* with a zest for life like nothing I'd ever seen.

After supper, Ollie explained my future to me. "Princess," she said, pointing to a newspaper photo of the valedictorian of the Class of '62. "This is going to be you." The girl had a pageboy and a pug nose. Her name was Margaret Smith. "She was homecoming queen too," Ollie said. "Nothing could stop her. And nothing will stop you." She folded the paper respectfully and filed it with her recipes. "Come," Ollie said. "Let's go get an ice cream cone. I'll introduce you to the neighbors." She took my hand. A wide, wincing smile was frozen on my face. I pulled my hand back.

"Ollie," I said.

"Yes, Daughter."

"When can Daughter have bangs?"

I sat in a kitchen chair with a towel clipped at the neck to cover my shoulders. Ollie combed the front half of my hair forward over my face and chopped straight across the forehead. Six inches of thin brown hair the texture of steel wool fell on the linoleum floor. Ollie took a deep breath and blew hard right in my face to get the itchy fine bits of hair off my skin. Instant bangs. My deformity was hidden. She combed the rest of my hair to either side and snipped it straight at chin level. Instant bob. I looked in the mirror. Between the horn-rims, the boobs, the bangs, and the bob, I was ready to meet the people I'd known all my life.

I had heard Sister Anne distinctly tell Ollie to keep my IQ under her hat. Ollie could no more keep my IQ under her hat than she could say a long grace. It became part of our introductions. "This is Princess," Ollie said, smiling down at my brain as we encountered Mr. Tanner walking the Doberman. "She's a genius."

The dog strained at his leash, wagging his tail madly, barking the wild, joyful bark of reunion. He was sure it was me. He wanted to break free, run over, and stick his snout in my behind. "How very nice to meet you, Mr. Tanner," I said as prompted. My face was contorted with a friendly grimace.

"Nice to meet you too, Princess," Mr. Tanner said.

When he had passed, Ollie filled me in. Mr. Tanner's two sons were away at Scout camp. They were nice, but they were both too young to be my boyfriend.

In the bait shop, we chose our flavors. Ollie got maple walnut, I got mint chip. Mr. Fanelli's eyes lingered on mine as he counted out our change into Ollie's palm, but he couldn't place me. We sat on the bait shop porch, licking our cones. Ollie pointed at the scar on the ground where our shack used to be. Between long, contented licks of ice cream, she divulged the seedy, grotesque tidbits parsed out at Bridge Night concerning me and the people who raised me.

"Derelicts," Ollie said. "Name of Cavanaugh. Had rats. The size of cats. Princess—they starved their own children." I listened guiltily, licking my cone, my spirit sinking into the water like a stone. The truth we were unable to utter ourselves was known and effortlessly repeated by everyone.

"Fella there hustled pool," Ollie said. "Got kicked out of gospel work for bigamy. Had a wife and another set of kids in Arkansas this wife here never knew about. Bragged about it down at the pool hall.

"This wife here he must have got out of a lunatic asylum. Never combed her hair. Thin as a stick. Never came out of that dump for seventeen years. Not 'til the day the fella next door killed himself. She went berserk. Went creeping around the Tanners' house foaming at the mouth, peeping in screens, screeching about the Kingdom of Heaven or some such. Right here in Iowa," Ollie said. "That's what gets me."

I couldn't resist. "Ollie?"

"Yes, Princess."

"Why'd that fella kill himself?"

"Got mixed up with the prostitute lived there," Ollie said. "She got him hooked on drugs. Or he got her hooked. I forget which. He overdosed, almost died. His wife found him. She called an ambulance. They pumped his stomach or some such. He broke it off with the prostitute. But she was already pregnant by him. Guess what the baby came out like?"

"Deformed, Ollie?"

"Yes, Princess. Blind, retarded, and deformed. She looked like a monster. Princess, she ate her own shit."

We both licked our cones. Mine tasted like shit. "Ollie?"

"Yes, Princess."

"What happened to the monster?"

"They took her away. She's being raised in an institution for people like her." We licked our cones. "I don't know why he killed himself," Ollie said.

At home, I culled the Arnold telephone book, looking for Cavanaughs, finding none.

"Princess," Ollie said that night, kneeling at my bedside.

"Yes, Ollie."

"I gotta come clean with you." In the darkness, I froze. What now? "I exaggerated on my application. I ain't all that much of a Methodist. We don't actually go to church. Ray thinks it's a waste of time. So if it's all the same to you, I won't pretend to say prayers with you. I'll leave you to do that on your own."

"Yes, Ollie."

"May the Lord bless you and keep you," she said. "That's all I aim to say." She kissed me on the forehead, right on the deformity, without even noticing.

———

Besides meals made from cans, we had meat. We fried pork chops in Ollie's GE electric skillet and ate them with apple-sauce on the side. We grilled steak. We baked potatoes, slicing them neatly from end to end, piling on sour cream and chives. We had all the things that would pass muster should Grace Paludy surprise us with a modern menu bust during the dinner hour, but Grace Paludy never did. My accomplishments surprised me instead. A variety of exciting new letters were showing up—B, F, K, P, Fe, Cd, and even Mg.

Sharing Ollie's food allowed me to share Ollie's assumptions. The stars still glittered in the depths of the heavens at this end of the lake, but we didn't go outside to watch them shift in their constellations ever so slowly across the night sky. We got our bearings from inside things, things bought from stores. Besides our clothes and our food, we defined ourselves with upholstery. We went shopping for a new club chair to coordinate with our olive sofa. We settled on one with a stripe that picked up the green.

I was free to run around our yard with a butterfly net all summer, catching and labeling butterflies. Sometimes I followed one across three backyards and up the bank to the railroad tracks. I stood in disoriented amazement, looking down at the point on the horizon where the parallel tracks met. There was the white X of the railroad crossing sign next to where our shack used to be. Vines grew up the side of the pharmacist's house. Someone had left his garage door open.

When I slept, I forgot where I was. I woke up in my pink bedroom, amazed at my comfort and cleanliness. Ollie would be in the kitchen setting a place at the table for me, a box of Kellogg's Corn Flakes open and ready, a carton of Iowa milk, a bowl of bananas exactly ripe. The morning sun would be peeping in through our kitchen window. The radio would be softly on so Ollie could find out quick-like if anyone had been killed or murdered. I became deeply attached to the smell of our life. Our cleanser was Pine-Sol. Our detergent was Tide. Our shampoo was Prell.

I smelled like the girls of Lake Mary. I remembered digging for night crawlers with Jima on August evenings when two of the girls of Lake Mary broke their parents' strict rules to

stay home and snuck down to the bait shop to flirt with Little
Duck. I could smell them coming for a hundred yards. They
came around the bend of the southern shore, smelling impos-
sibly clean from head to toe. The parts in their clean hair were
straight. Their ears looked brand-new. Their elbows were soft
and pink with no folds, no dirt stains. Their shorts looked new
and stiff in pink, yellow, green, or blue. Their blouses were con-
temporary, modern prints with jazzy drawings of ordinary things
placed upside down and sideways. I could smell their hair spray,
their shampoo, their hand cream, their lipstick, their soap, and
their perfume. They were so clean and well formed, I wanted
to bite their legs. Not break the skin or anything, just sink my
teeth into their calves enough to leave a small impression.

They used to pass within a foot of Little Duck, keeping
their eyes straight ahead, not looking at him. "Hi," he'd say,
knowing they had come all this way to get his attention just so
they could snub him. They walked past, eyes front, along the
marina. Little Duck would crouch there, cleaning engine parts
in kerosene, knowing they'd be back. They walked awhile,
then talked awhile, and when they returned, strolling past the
marina to the bait shop again, he would be ready. There sat
the can of kerosene by itself in the dirt with the brush inside,
handle sticking out. In the shade of the trees where we were
digging for night crawlers, leaning against the bark, was Little
Duck, smoking a cigarette, his shirt open, his legs crossed at the
ankle, his eyes on the tips of his engineer boots. In the evening
light, he was the color of a Hollywood hero, so graceful, so
calm, so cool.

The girls looked at the empty place where they expected
to see him, crouching over engine parts, manly and skilled.

They were disappointed and agitated. They were sullen and insecure. The dullness of a summer night in Lake Mary with no sex symbol in sight oppressed them. The vacancy of life stretched before them interminably. They wondered if their beauty, their fragrance, their perfection were wasted out here, tonight and possibly forever.

Then they saw him, leaning against the tree with his shirt open, smoking, muscles dusky, jaw in shadow. Their breath caught in their throats. Jima and me looked at each other, cracking very small smiles.

"Hel-*lo*," Little Duck said.

"Oh, hi," they both said, competing with each other to smile the prettier, sexier smile, each one hoping Little Duck would look at her longer than the other. If he did, they couldn't quite tell, which made him irresistible, which made them come back the next possible night.

To smell like they smelled seemed an impossibility back then, but now I did. I thrived on our cleanliness and our routine. I liked sharing the evening meal with a man and a woman at the dinette table, Ray behind the newspaper, Ollie at the can opener. The sound of that little motor grinding its blades into the lid of an aluminum can soothed and oriented me. I liked my evening bath with Ivory soap and a thick, white towel. I liked sitting all clean afterward in our living room watching TV with Ollie and Ray. Most of all, I liked love. Loyal to the point of death, pure, strong, and uncomplicated, the love of Ollie Hopkins rained gently down on me every hour. It even possessed the telltale quality of delusion: Ollie took excessive delight in my physical appearance. Those moist eyes, that smitten smile, that quickening of emotion in her chest when

I came charging into the living room, looking like Benjamin Franklin with bangs and a bob, proved that the love of a true mother, adoptive or not, is blind.

"May the Lord bless you and keep you," Ollie would say when she tucked me in. She would kiss my forehead. She closed my bedroom door, and she and Ray would argue lightly about me.

"Since you got her, you forgot about me," Ray would say. "All you care about is her."

"I care about you," Ollie would say. But I could hear in her tone that she *had* forgotten about him. All she *did* care about was me. She must have done something romantic next.

"That's more like it," Ray would say.

I would wait until 9:49. Then I'd climb out of bed and go to the window to watch for the train that never came. They'd closed the route. Out of loyalty, I stood there, trying to bear witness to my old life with my sister and brother. But when I tried, it never worked. The emotion that had been building up inside all day evaporated. Our old reality seemed unreal. It had to come at me on its own terms, sidelong, like a surprise assault, a flood of forbidden associations, eroding my confidence in my new life and my disguise. It had to come like a hallucination when I least expected it, a soft cotton yellowness approaching in my peripheral vision, quickening my heart with its compelling reality, its disorienting sorrow. And when it came, I froze.

In the Arnold yellow pages under Automobile Repair, there were only four garages. The street addresses were abbreviated. *Msker. Lndn. Sthbry. Mn. Mn* was Main—that was where Ollie and I got our gas. My heart often thudded as I waited in the passenger seat, hoping irrationally to see Little Duck amble out from the cool darkness of the garage to pump our high-test. But it was always J. P., a man with huge, careful, ruined hands. His nails were black and cracked. Quaker State oil was deeply etched in the lines of his palms. He flirted with Ollie, making her blush.

At home, when Ray mentioned cars, my ears perked up. I ran over to give him my full attention, hoping that would make him draw out the story. But Ray's stories were one sentence long no matter what. So-and-so got a royal screwing on an engine job. Someone else got sideswiped, but the bodywork was so good the car looked new. I listened hard for a name, a street, for any hint, any tint of Little Duck Cavanaugh. Nothing.

—

I'd lived here a month and Grace Paludy had managed to never officially meet me. We sometimes encountered her in the evening, walking down the driveway to her aqua Ford station wagon as we were returning from the bait shop. She was heading down to the Methodist church to rehearse the organ for Sunday. Mrs. Paludy had a figure like a telephone booth. She made it more so by wearing a blocky dress that fell straight from her shoulders to her knee. Her mouth was straight and humorless. She ran over it with lipstick, creating a red equals sign. The only thing round or soft about her was the bulge on her left side. Ollie had warned me not to look at it. A piece of her colon had squirted out between sections of muscle. It jiggled. I couldn't keep my eyes off it. Even worse, I wanted to touch it. "Evening, Grace," Ollie would say when we were within a few feet of each other.

Grace had the snob's ability to angle her head slightly away from you, fixing her eyes on an important event in her immediate future that so concerned her, it prevented her from hearing human speech regardless of its proximity. She got into her aqua wagon and drove away. It irked Ollie. "They speak, but she don't," she said to Ray at night as we three sat together on the sofa, watching television. It was true. Her husband and his three sons waved and called hello to us several times a day. They were tall, wholesome, athletic men with blue eyes and white teeth. They often had a baseball game going in the backyard. They played basketball using the hoop on the garage. It was as if the Paludy men were a separate clan.

Ray always said the same thing. "She ain't worthy to lick your shoes."

One evening when Ollie saw Mrs. Paludy open the back door and walk down the driveway, she took my hand. We humped outside and blocked access to Grace's car. "Grace," Ollie said, "I'd like you to meet my daughter, Princess. She's a genius."

"How do you do, dearie," Grace said without looking at me.

"Just fine, sweetheart," I said. Ollie had accidentally taught me to revile the woman.

Ollie and I had our first fight. "How could you!" she said, back in our kitchen. "I'm trying so hard to prove we're cultured people. Now she'll tell everyone we're coarse." Ray had lowered his newspaper. For the first time, he was happy with me.

"I'm sorry, Ollie," I said.

That night when we were watching television, a slapstick orchestra played the "Hawaiian War Chant." Three girl singers in straw skirts sang the song, first in Hawaiian, then in English.

I jumped off the sofa and stood next to the television to show
Ollie and Ray the war hula I learned from Mrs. Sodstrum.

> Ta-hu-wa-i-la-a ta-hu-wa-i-wa-i,
> e-hu-he-ne-la-a-pi-li-ko-o-lu-a-la
> pu-tu-tu-i-lu-a-i-te-to-e-la,
> ha-nu-li-po-i-e-ta-pa-a-lai.
> Au we ta hu-a la
> Au we ta hu-a la.

I got the *hooleilei* right, arms straight out in front, palms
out, hips swaying from side to side. Once I had that going, I
broke out into the side step. On the chorus, I wiggled my hips,
waving both arms gently to the side. Back to the *hooleilei* for
the English verse.

> There's a sunny little funny little melody
> That was started by a native down in Wai ki ki
> He would gather a crowd down beside the sea
> And they'd play his gay Hawaiian chant:
> Ow-way-tah-hoo-ah lah.
> Me big bad fightin' man.

For the grand finale, I did the hop, crouching down and
hopping forward with my knees bent, still gesturing (though
not as gracefully as Mrs. Sodstrum) with my hands. I hopped
back, stood up, and let my hips go wild (though not as wild
as Mrs. Sodstrum). Ray was laughing his soundless laugh, his
shoulders shaking spasmodically, his eyes squinted shut. That
made twice in one night that he'd gotten a kick out of me.

Ollie was inspired. "Daughter," she said, "you are going to knock them dead on Bridge Night." It was our turn to host next. She bought the 45.

—

We dusted and vacuumed the living room, then filled it with card tables. For our menu, we avoided Mrs. Tanner's mistake. Her Cheese Nut Balls were too rich. Everyone said so—not to her face, but in the driveway. Instead, we made Bridge Mix. "Melt six tablespoons margarine," Ollie read. We added Lawry's Seasoned Salt and Worcestershire sauce. "Stir in Corn Chex, Rice Chex, and Wheat Chex," Ollie read. The last ingredient was the best. "Add one cup mixed nuts," Ollie read. The luxury of this was unfathomable. "Mix well," she read. I did.

"Get the tongs, Daughter," Ollie said.

"What are tongs?" I said.

Ollie was happy when she had a chance to teach me things she'd just learned. "When you have people over nice-like," Ollie said, "you bring everything you need out into the living room. So when your guests come in, you ask them, *How's tricks*, and fix them a drink without never leaving their presence."

I watched from my bedroom window as our neighbors left their homes in Lake Mary and walked up the shore road to our front door. They'd dressed up, altering their appearances subtly so that they seemed like newer, more colorful, more uncomfortable versions of their daily selves. Except for Grace Paludy. Same straight, dull chemise, same red equals sign over her lips.

I took everyone's coats to the master bedroom when Ollie asked me to. I brought everyone cocktail napkins when theirs sailed to the floor. Everyone again told Ollie I was polite. Except Grace Paludy.

They sat down to play. With a name like bridge, I expected their card game to look interesting, but the interesting part must have been going on in their minds. I went to my room to change. I rubbed rouge in my cheeks. I drew lipstick over my lips.

Ollie was tipsy when she came to get me. I realized too late that doing the hula for tipsy Lake Mary people on Bridge Night was a bad idea. I hung my head as she led me out of my room and down the hall. Everyone snickered when they saw me. Imagine Benjamin Franklin in a muumuu and grass skirt. Ollie put on the 45.

Here came the opening eight drumbeats of the "Hawaiian War Chant." As the three women sang it, I did a feeble *hooleilei*. Everyone laughed, Mrs. Paludy the loudest.

> Ta-hu-wa-i-la-a ta-hu-wa-i-wa-i,
> e-hu-he-ne-la-a-pi-li-ko-o-lu-a-la

On the chorus, I wiggled my hips, waving both arms gently to the side. Everyone was in hysterics, Mrs. Paludy the most.

> Ow-way-tah-hoo-ah lah.
> Me big bad fightin' man.

They were laughing so loud I couldn't hear the King sisters. I lost the beat. I stood there waiting for the song to end, my head hanging, my arms dangling uselessly, the bottom of one bare foot pressing into the top of the other, the way girls did when they wished they could disappear through a hole in the floor. Ollie realized they were laughing *at* me. She took the needle off.

"She didn't do the hop," Ray said.

"Ray, honey," Ollie said.

"They want to see the hop," Ray said. "The hop is the best part."

"Ray, honey," Ollie said. "Another time."

"Tell her to do it again and do the God damn hop," he said. Our neighbors were embarrassed. They made small, impatient noises, wishing the evening could somehow go back to the way it was right before Ray said *God damn*. They started clearing their throats, shaking the ice in their highball glasses, stretching their legs, keeping their eyes on their shoes.

Ollie put the needle on the record. I did it all over again, ending with the hop, crouching down as low as I could go, hopping forward, knees bent, gesturing with my hands, then hopping back. I lost my balance, falling over backward. Everyone saw my underpants. I jumped upright for the finale, my hips gyrating a little bit. Everyone except Mrs. Paludy clapped loud and hard. They meant it. I'd been a good sport.

I slunk down the hall to my room. "Ray. *Friend*," I heard Terrance Tanner say. "Not to butt in. But that wasn't necessary."

"Look," Ray said, as if he was honor-bound to lay down the law established by his forefathers for generations. "*You don't show people a hula and leave out the hop.*"

When everyone had said good night and gone home, Ollie formed a fist with her right hand and pumped it hard in the air, taking aim. "Ollie'd like to brain that Grace Paludy with her stuck-up busted colon," she said. "She never clapped once."

"She ain't worthy to lick your shoes," Ray said to Ollie. "Yours either," he said to me, proving I was one of the family.

———

Ollie and I both loved thunderstorms. One hot August evening, we got trapped down at the bait shop in the middle of one. The humidity had been building up since dawn, slowly saturating the air with pressure. The sun was harsh and hot, shining so hard that we thought it could never rain again. Every hour, more humidity pumped itself into the air. By late afternoon, it was so humid we could talk of nothing else. Suddenly, a cloud passed over the sun. Instead of hot fresh sweat pouring off our arms, the sweat we already had began to dry and cool. The air filled with pressure, collecting and sorting itself into two incompatible kinds of electricity. We knew any minute we would hear that first delicious crackle of thunder on the distant horizon, a sound like God crumpling paper. We strolled down to the bait shop. *Kkkkkkkkkkk.* There it was. Ollie and I looked at each other. We shivered with pleasure. We both loved thunder. Another crackle, closer. We slipped into the bait shop and bought our cones. Wham-o. Thunder crashed straight overhead, tickling our inner ears and shooting a slow wave of sensation down our spines all the way to our toes. We stood on the bait shop porch and watched, enjoying the downpour covering Iowa for a hundred miles. And with every thunderclap, we got goose bumps. We licked our cones, our eyes dilated.

"Looking out at cornfields always gives me peace," Ollie said to me. "Reminds me a home. I loved farm life. I was nine when I got polio. Woke up one day and couldn't walk. Now they got a vaccine prevents it. But oh, how miserable and useless I felt, lying there paralyzed when Pappy—I called him Pappy, he was my granddad—when Pappy needed me down in the barn." Ollie could say in the rain personal things she wouldn't say in the sunshine. I was getting her true life story. How I wished I could tell her mine. She was just getting started when Ray pulled up in the green Plymouth, honking long and hard. He'd driven down to save us from the storm. We thanked him over and over the way he expected us to, so he would never guess he'd ruined it.

—

Ollie wanted my entry into public school to be smooth and socially successful. One of the advantages of raising a girl was social involvement. She dreamed of being the center of attention as the girls of Lake Mary clamored to play with me. She imagined us all baking cookies together or boiling homemade syrup for popcorn balls. She would be the most popular mother among the girls. The other mothers would wonder what her secret was. They'd want to get to know her better.

At Bridge Night, Ollie had heard other mothers discuss their daughters' slumber parties. She planned one for me. We picked out invitations. We shopped for Fritos and Coke. We bought party favors and board games, then played them ourselves when, one by one, the girls called to cancel, sick or indisposed. I was relieved. I feared close scrutiny. I thanked my lucky stars that Ollie was as off-putting as me. What a team we made—Ollie with her farmer forthrightness and one calf the size of a broomstick, me always socially paralyzed, freezing in place. People steered clear of us.

—

Sunday mornings at nine, Ollie tuned the television to the church service of the evangelist Dr. Paige Jiggins. Ollie didn't tune in Paige Jiggins to worship. She tuned him in to see how stupid most people can be. The deacon sailed out from behind the curtains to warm up the crowd. It was Big Duck without a hat. He took the pulpit to greet us, the television audience. "There's a phony for you," Ollie said. The shiver of truth intertwined with a pleasurable disloyalty in me.

Big Duck's suit was costly. It fit like a glove. His glittering black eyes, gleaming black hair, and very white, straight false teeth were photogenic. His aura of quiet power had become noisy. There was his jaw taking charge of the television audience. People submitted to it. They looked to it for redemption and approval, and that meant emptying their pockets. He talked nonsense now, making a direct cause-and-effect connection between a person's capacity to convert others to the new Faith Movement and an increase in personal wealth.

Paige Jiggins took the microphone. "Here comes Scallywag Number One," Ollie said. He was better looking than Big Duck. He had a high, shiny forehead and electrode eyes that came straight out of the television to stun you like headlights. If Big Duck's suit fit good, his fit better. If Big Duck preached long, he preached longer. If Duck's voice was loud, Dr. Jiggins's was louder, thundering with heartfelt humility. Dr. Jiggins had the air of a man with extra testosterone who used it to con you, assuming that if he was entertaining enough in the process, he would eventually be forgiven. Behind him, Big Duck had the air of a man who wouldn't.

Any minute, I expected Tit to make her appearance, glittering and phosphorescent, a cross in her cleavage, wielding her

gospel-y contralto like a love club. I was hyperventilating, sucking in Os. Instead, here came Miss Katy, a tidy woman deacon
with conventional looks in the Mary Tyler Moore vein, handing out prayer cards to the studio audience. When Big Duck led
the audience in a medley of hymns that had been updated with
a rock and roll beat, Miss Katy joined him at the microphone.
They stood side by side, making eye contact as they sang like
Sonny and Cher. *I got you, babe.* So much for Tit.

Dr. Jiggins devoted a great portion of his sermon to describ-
ing his own wonders. Ollie turned to me. "Princess," she said,
"you were raised by nuns. Did you ever once hear Jesus brag?"
There was Dr. Jiggins citing chapter and verse: his revival was
simulcast on four hundred television stations; he routinely sat
eighteen thousand people; he estimated his radio and television audiences at almost one billion, the largest ministry in the
world. This week he was happy to unveil in the chapel at Christ
Town a beautiful new twelve-foot-high cross encrusted with
semiprecious jewels. Ollie turned to me. "Princess," she said,
"did Jesus say one word about jewels?"

Dr. Jiggins had more to say. His education center had forty
classrooms now; the retirement center had a hundred beds. Yet,
his campus was only half complete. More dollars were needed.
He wanted to build a hospital, so that more miraculous healings could be bestowed. Ollie turned to me. "What do they
need a hospital for if people are healed?" she said.

Dr. Jiggins held up his monthly magazine, asking the television viewers to subscribe. On the cover were three men in
white doctor's coats, all endorsing the medical legitimacy of
the healings of Dr. Paige Jiggins. "Ollie will give you a million
dollars," Ollie said to me, "if any of them are real doctors."

Today, Dr. Jiggins was pleased to announce a wonderful blessing: Billy Graham was welcoming him to lead the opening prayer at the World Congress on Evangelism, a historical first. Too long, too long, he said, there had been tension between those devoted to the teachings of Christ who differed ever so slightly on the issue of the practice of the gifts of the Holy Spirit.

"Friends," Paige Jiggins said, and his whole face burned brighter as he preached. "You can control everything great and powerful, including Satan, with your own tongue. Your mind and your tongue contain supernatural ability and power. When you speak, you produce a divine force that will heal, that will produce wealth, that will bring success, that will influence the environment.

"God automatically does what you command when you positively confess your desires in faith. The spirit world can be operated by you through supernatural laws. It is the first and foremost spiritual law; words are the most powerful thing in the universe. Go forth and bring the light to those who surround you. If you Christians don't abide by and operate spiritual laws successfully, then God Himself is hindered in His ability to act in your life and in the lives of others.

"How many people are here today who claim to uphold the principles of the Faith Movement—but for whom the principles don't seem to be working? Theirs is a faith based on misunderstanding. Those people are confessing, not commanding. It was Jesus who brought Christians the commanding power. It was Jesus who promised you if you have faith in Him, you can have whatever you say."

"Princess," Ollie said, "did you ever hear such a load of b.s. in your life?"

Contributions were flowing in over the phone right in front of Ollie and me. Paige Jiggins was so grateful for these blessings, his eyes teared up. He thanked God the Father, the Son, and the Holy Spirit. His eyes rolled back in his head. He spoke in tongues. It was all I could do to keep from showing Ollie how much better I was at it than him.

—

My clean pillowcases smelled like Tide. Moonlight brightened the dark corners of my room. Ollie was tucking me in. "Do you remember anything about your scalding?" she asked after kissing my forehead. I froze. We'd just seen an episode of *The Twilight Zone* about a girl who'd forgotten she'd witnessed a crime as a child, then suffered a special kind of amnesia that kept drawing her back to the scene of the crime, putting her in mortal danger—the criminal haunted the crime scene too.

"No, Ollie," I said.

"If you ever saw that wicked nanny again," Ollie said, "would you recognize her?" Sister Anne had coached me to answer every question of this type with a simple *I don't know*. But I looked at Ollie's loyal features in the moonlight and I wanted to enjoy this moment to the fullest. I ignored Sister Anne's advice.

"Yes, Ollie," I said.

"If you ever want to return to Adel to see if anything there rings a bell," Ollie said, "just say so. I will drive you." Her features contracted and hardened, growing formidable and warlike. "But if you saw a woman walking down the street there, and you said, *Ollie, that's her*, I just might stop the car and strangle her. I know the Ten Commandments: *Thou Shalt Not*

Kill. But when I think about what was done to you," Ollie said, "I can just feel that woman's throat under my thumbs. Let her gag and spit and say, *Please, please, please.* Princess, I might not be able to stop myself. I got strength in my arms from farm life and I might just use it to kill her. I'd go to jail and you'd have to finish raising yourself 'til I got out. Is she a big woman?"

I shook my head no. Ollie seemed pleased. In the moonlight, Ollie's features settled back into their normal, peaceful expression. She stood up in stages, testing her balance before she could shift her weight to her bad leg. She skipped her usual benediction. "Good night, Princess," she said, walking toward the door.

"Good night, Mother," I said without thinking.

Ollie did a double take, looking over her shoulder at me with moist, smitten eyes to see if she'd heard me correctly. "Princess," she said, "what'd you say?"

I clapped my hand over my mouth. In my excitement at Ollie's pledge of physical protection, I'd broken her rule. "I'm sorry, Ollie," I said a hundred times as she limped over to my bedside to hug me and cry.

—

The evening air was getting cooler. Ollie and I put on sweatshirts to stroll down to the bait shop for ice cream. The Tanner brothers were home from Scout camp. They came riding down the shore road on bicycles. They rode up to meet us, stopping with their hands on the handlebars, one foot on the sidewalk and one on the pedal. Bobby was still all business, introducing them both, referring to himself as Robert. Cooper was tan. His hair was sun-bleached. His brown eyes were still daydreamy

and artistic. His voice was still husky and sweet. Ollie introduced us. "How long have you lived here?" Cooper asked me.

I stood in the gathering dusk afraid to speak, thinking
my voice might give me away. My crush was rekindled. For
months, I'd hulaed for him. And here he was. *Aloha au la oe.*
Ollie nudged me. "Ten weeks." I said it so soft, Ollie had to
repeat it for me.

—

To shop for school clothes, the department store on Main Street
in Arnold was not considered fashionable enough for Princess.
Ollie and I tied scarves under our chins and drove to Diamond's
in Des Moines. Diamond's was six stories high and took up a
whole city block. To park, we had to drive up a great concrete
spiral ramp and look for an empty space between painted white
parallel lines. Inside, the store smelled like wealth—perfume,
oiled wood, and fine cloth. Diamond's lifted the whole idea of
needing things up a few notches. You didn't come here to quickly
grab a few necessities. You came here to be someone new. There
were lovely things guaranteed to transform you, designed
and manufactured by famous designers with that new you in
mind. Words like *cashmere, 100% silk, imported from London*
were leisurely uttered by soft-voiced clerks whose appearances
achieved an air of prosperity that had to be false, or why would
they be clerks? The marvels began with the escalator, silently
rising in the middle of the store to the next floor. We stepped
on board and rose in place, twisting reflectively to survey the
quiet, gleaming counters from above. We rode up three floors
to Separates. In magazines, Ollie had seen the sweatered look
for fall in softer, care-free Orlon. And here it was in Diamond's.

We both got matching sets. Ollie chose coral. I chose tangerine. The marvels continued with Ollie's charge account. Instead of counting out dollars, she just signed her name—a little self-consciously, perhaps, her big tongue in the corner of her mouth, trying to make her large, round, halting penmanship stay on the line instead of sliding diagonally down the charge slip. "Thank you, Mrs. Hopkins," the clerk said.

———

And so it was with melodramatic self-consciousness, as Princess Hopkins with her black horn-rims, her bangs, and her bob, looking like Benjamin Franklin with boobs in a tangerine care-free Orlon sweater set, I walked down the shore road to board the yellow bus for the first day of public school.

I found my homeroom. I was assigned a seat. Just before the tardy bell rang, Jump Wicket sauntered through the door. He was back from a year in juvenile detention and he'd flunked two grades. The teacher seated him next to me. Discomfort led to helplessness, helplessness led to shame, shame led to fear, and fear to pain—this time the flood of hormones I excreted was lost on him. I forced myself to breathe and tried not to pant. His clothes were worn and out of style. Mine were expensive and new. His hair was shaggy. He needed new shoes. No one was afraid of him anymore. It seemed too many boys had caught up with him in height and strength. The blankness that had inhabited him as a nine-year-old, replacing any organized personality, was now, at fourteen, a wind tunnel of impotent self-loathing.

I found the reversal in social status between us overstimulating. The way Jump moved through a throng of his peers during passing periods, emanating hollow, worthless detachment like a convict in training, touched me deeply. I could feel him approaching when he was still halfway down the hall. He would saunter into homeroom and drop into his seat. Within sixty seconds, he would look over at my tits to see if they looked bigger today or smaller—sometimes the things I wore created an optical illusion. That was the full extent of his awareness of me. Vivid memories of the intensity of his attention as he ordered me to do things in the reeds combined with irrational nostalgia for my lost life in the shack to render me secretly, shamefully in love. I closed my eyes to inhale his smell.

—

Finally, science! Here in the sun-filled windows of the laboratory on the second floor of Abraham Lincoln High School began my devoted apprenticeship to Ted Fonic, the science teacher. Ted Fonic was a lean, overeducated man with pale red eyebrows, green eyes, and a receding hairline. His clothes, based on television shows I'd seen, linked him to universities in the East—lightweight tweed sports jackets, ascots, and slacks. He wore loafers with tassels, and, when he lectured, he walked back and forth in front of us with the poise and bearing of a ballet dancer. He wore a gold ring on his finger, but either his wife had died or fled or she never existed. He made it clear he lived alone.

Ted Fonic taught biology, physics, and chemistry. Imagine how I felt when he reached up to pull down the large, shiny, retractable chart he called the periodic table of the elements. I disrupted class by laughing uncontrollably. There, arrayed before me, each with a name, an atomic number, an atomic weight, and a class, were the symbols for every material thing on earth and in space, from actinium to zirconium, symbols that I'd been shitting for years. "Anything that has mass and takes up space is made from one or more of these elements," he said to us. "Some occur in nature. Some are man-made. Some are common. Some are rare. Over ninety-eight percent of the earth is made up of eight of these elements. Can anyone guess what the most common element is?" He called on me.

"Oxygen," I said.

———

Socially, I succeeded in disappointing Ollie. Each day after school, she waited breathlessly for me to report invitations to football games, dances, movies, or mixers from boys who were motivated by the cuteness of my outfits. There were none. She tried to coach me. "If some fella says to you, *Say, that science class was hard*, all you got to say is, *Come on over to my house and I'll help you with the homework.*"

Each morning at the breakfast table when she looked at me dressed for school, hope dawned anew. Her eyes would grow misty with approval as if imagining how irresistible I'd appear to the boys at Abraham Lincoln High School. "Princess," Ollie would say, "I have a feeling today is your day." I'd board the bus, walk down the aisle to the last row, and sit by the window, reading a book. I succeeded at being lost in the shuffle. Both boys and girls steered clear of me. My looks were strange, my manner off-putting. Everyone quickly got sick of teachers making a big deal when they handed me back my tests, praising me for a perfect score.

I threw myself into assisting Ted Fonic. It didn't seem right that a man with a mind as fine as his would be consigned to menial labor as a consequence of choosing to educate public school students, but that was the case. The girl in charge of the hamster cage let it get so dirty that the hamster stopped using the exercise wheel. His eyes grew dull. He gained a pound. I couldn't stand to see refined Ted Fonic sifting through soiled straw to discard hamster shit. I did it. One of the boys in the physics class turned the ripple tank on high until it broke. Everyone failed the standardized test on wave motion. I sat down with Mr. Fonic after school to learn small-engine repair. The janitor stumbled into our tray of four hundred unnumbered biology slides meant to teach the sequence of cell development. I picked them up off the floor and sat side by side with Mr. Fonic, holding them up to the window light to identify the order of each one, accidentally learning a year's worth of biology in the process.

—

One stormy afternoon when the gym teacher called in sick, we were left sitting around the polished floor of the gym with nothing to do but listen to thunder. A strange mood came over us girls, attuning us, making us of one mind. Someone started to tell the story of me and the people who raised me. "Remember the poor kids who lived in the shack?" she said. "They were so poor they had nothing to eat. They had nothing to wear. They barely had heat. Never had a bicycle. Never had a Christmas tree. They were raised by two women and a man who kept them out of school. They couldn't read or write. One of the women used to come into town to turn tricks. She always went to see the druggist.

"The oldest kid, the boy, he was the only normal one," she said. "God, he was cute. All the girls had crushes on him. He looked like James Dean. But he was white trash. The two little girls—they were ugly as sin. They were retarded. One was blind. All they were fit to do was sell worms." Everyone thought about that. Especially me.

"The druggist got on drugs that made him go berserk. He got a gun. His wife was afraid of him. She went home to live with her mother. He took the gun and killed himself."

"Why?" someone said. It might have been me.

"Drugs make you do that," the girl said. "Sometimes you rob people and kill them. Sometimes you just kill yourself." *Just*, I thought.

"Then what happened?" someone said, even though they all knew.

"The man in the shack took off with the women and the county put the retarded girls in a home." Everyone was quiet, thinking about the sad end of the poor kids who used to live in the shack.

"What happened to the normal kid?" someone asked. It might have been me.

"He's still in town, fixing cars," the girl said. "He's married now. He has two kids." *But no phone*, I thought.

"Remember what happened next?" the girl said.

They all did remember. "Tell us," they said.

"People kept complaining about the rats up there. Finally the town came over with a bulldozer. And when they razed the shack, they found a human skeleton." All the girls looked at each other with eyes made round and wide with horror. I did too. "One of the women did not take off with the man after all. She hid herself away in there without food or water 'til she died." Everyone got the willies. Especially me.

"And now, when the moon is full," the girl said. "If you look down where the shack used to be, the moonlight shines off the lake onto those old concrete pilings and makes a mirage. It looks like the shack is still there." Everyone had seen it but me.

———

I succumbed to the pull of my old life. Afternoons in late September, I would walk down the railroad tracks with my butterfly net over one shoulder as a ruse. I would sit on the railroad bank smoking a cigarette secretly bought from the bait shop vending machine when Ollie wasn't looking. I would gaze down into the reeds at Little Duck's overturned boat. Weather had bleached the wood white, though the black painted shadows of the boat's name were still legible—MMM GOOD. I could just see him loping down to the bait shop in his Levi's, his white shirttails flapping behind him, his tan chest winking out in front. I could just see Jima in the shadows of the trees down there, lip-syncing Fats Domino. *You made* (dum-dum). *Me cry* (dum-dum). The raw scar in the ground where the shack once stood stymied me like an unsolvable math problem. Two rooms and a woodstove. How had six people fit in there, let alone fought?

The FOR SALE sign in front of the pharmacist's house had fallen and rotted into the ground. No one wanted to buy a house where a man could kill himself. I crushed out my cigarette and walked down the railroad bank. In my father's backyard there was still a pool of cool molecules where his soul rolled around. I walked through it deliberately on my way to study *Camponotus pennsylvanicus*, his carpenter ants.

C. pennsylvanicus was a black carpenter, ranging in size from one-half to three-quarters of an inch. Most of the workers worked what I called the Tanner Trail, a lengthy, well-established route that led from a large outdoor nest to the Tanners' garbage pail. Someone in that household liked oranges enough to buy them, but not enough to finish them. They left that to the ants. I admired the efficiency of ants, jerking along in a multisegmented, calculatingly angled, unvarying path from their tidy, beautifully organized nest to a permanent food supply.

A less-traveled trail led from the garbage pail to my father's house. I followed. I could never enter there without sniffing the air madly for any vestige of my mother. It was musty and dank. Wood was rotting. Mold was forming. All the sour residues of decay drowned out any remaining molecular hint of Letitia Grund. I often stood in the living room for a moment, mesmerized by the simple sorrow of a dead console television. Facing it was a plaid upholstered chair that mice had made a nest in.

The carpenters zigzagged over the change in texture where the living room carpet gave way to the kitchen linoleum, bearing bits of food they'd foraged from the Tanners. They jerked toward the cabinet under the sink, found the water pipe, and climbed up, emerging into the sink basin out of the drain. From the sink it was a short distance across the counter to the windowsill. They climbed through a gap where the wood had warped to a nest they'd bored inside the window frame. From here, the smaller, younger carpenters made a shorter, simpler trip to a cupboard where a pool of honey had spilled years before.

—

Queens were the founders and rulers of the ant colony. A *Camponotus* queen could live for eighteen to twenty-nine years, I read in one of Ted Fonic's monthly entomology abstracts. These were written by experts based on the campus right here in Arnold at Iowa State University. Queens had wings and on these wings on warm days in early summer when they were ready to mate, they would fly away from the anthill. The males were excited but easygoing, following their winking queens on brief nuptial flights, mating, then conveniently dying. Other than mating, male ants did no work. In some colonies where not all males had wings, mating took place inside the natal nest instead of on the wing. It wasn't always violins and candlelight. The wingless males could become extremely aggressive, engaging in intense and often violent competition with the more docile winged males to mate with the virgin queen.

Once she had mated, the queen dug a new nest. She retreated deep inside, tearing off her wings, for she would never fly again. She began a life of egg-laying. The queen fed the tiny larvae with a fluid from her own body, tirelessly tending them so they would grow into fat white cocoons, also known as pupae. From these cocoons, like clockwork, worker ants emerged. The first generation was made up of workers that were small in size and timid, two features that helped them survive. Now the queen could stop feeding them and they could start feeding her.

Worker ants cared for the next generation of eggs laid by the queen, moving them carefully from one nursery to the next, sometimes taking them out into the warm sunlight for an afternoon airing. They possessed a gland above their hind legs that secreted a substance that functioned as an antibiotic, preventing bacteria or fungi from infecting the colony. Researchers had recently discovered a 92-million-year-old ant preserved in amber in New Jersey. They were particularly enthused because this ant possessed that gland. Without that gland, ants could not survive underground or in rotting trees, places where deadly bacteria are plentiful and could easily decimate an entire colony.

Queens founded new nests when a colony reached maturity. Maturity was a relative issue, differing greatly from species to species. Colonies of army ants were not considered mature until the worker population exceeded hundreds of thousands of individuals—or even a million. At the other extreme was a species of tiny fungus-growers who needed only thirty-five individuals to reach maturity. In between the army ants and the fungus grower was *C. pennsylvanicus*, whose colonies contained from nineteen hundred to twenty-five hundred members.

I had a question for Mr. Fonic. Now that the Tanners had two garbage pails, the ants on that trail had doubled in number. By contrast, the honey pool in the pharmacist's kitchen was almost gone. Was it a coincidence or a result that fewer ants followed the honey trail now, and those that did were farther apart? Who decided how many ants foraged for honey and how many ants foraged for fruit? Either someone in the colony had one heck of a brain for planning or they all did. Could ants talk? Mr. Fonic's green eyes were intrigued. He didn't have a long enough answer for me. We agreed to find out. We would establish an ant farm in the classroom and design experiments in ant communication.

Following the advice of Ted Fonic's colleagues, the entomologists at ISU, I chose the newest, least-developed hill. With a sharp spade, I dug all the way around, deep and straight. We didn't want to disturb the entire civilization without locating a queen. Workers went fleeing chaotically by the dozens. I found pupae. I found larvae. There she was, the queen, twice as big as all of them. What a thorax! Into my five-gallon bucket she went.

Ollie was ready with the science book open on the kitchen table. "Dissolve agar in boiling water," she said, reading out loud from the ant-food recipe. "Let cool. Stir one tablespoon honey into one cup distilled water. Mash multivitamin. Add pinch salt." We did all that. "Beat one egg. Combine ingredients. Stir until smooth." We fed the queen. She seemed grateful. She calmed right down. She was storing up her strength for the ordeals to come, without yet having to know what they were. That's what made her the queen.

Twice a week, Ollie made ant food. She could have handed me the jar in the morning when she kissed me good-bye. I could have carried it to school on the bus. Instead, she drove me and the jar there herself in order to case the halls for romantic prospects. "That tall fella with the big chin," she'd say when Harold Kwack walked by. "He's attractive." Harold Kwack was not only not attractive, he was undergoing psychological testing. He had drawn a cartoon of himself cutting up the girls' advisor into little pieces with a hatchet, then slipped the drawing under the door to her office. "That little kid with the blue shirt," Ollie would say when Nick Griffy walked by. "He smiled at you." Nick Griffy smiled at everything. He sniffed airplane glue in a brown paper bag in the boys' bathroom between classes. Ollie's instincts were off. She was infallibly drawn to the ineligible.

At Bridge Night, Ollie learned what other teenagers did to mingle. They had pizza parties where they danced to the new 45, "Surfin' USA." Ollie planned a pizza party at our house, calling all the mothers weeks ahead of time, buying the record, shopping for Coca-Cola and Bubble Up. The day arrived. We ordered the pizza in advance, a large pepperoni, then ate it ourselves when no one came. One by one, they called to cancel.

If Ollie could have just seen me for five minutes navigating the halls of Abraham Lincoln High School, everything would have been explained to her. Other kids moved easily together, in pairs, three abreast, or even in small gangs, talking, laughing, and flirting. Some boys jostled and shoved, punching each other's biceps playfully by way of a greeting. Other boys walked slowly with their arms around girls. Some girls gossiped brazenly in each other's ears, hiding their lips with the flat of a hand. Others tended each other, fixing clothes, makeup, and hair. I went hurtling down the hall alone in a direct path parallel to the wall like a bug-eyed troll who shopped at Diamond's, unspeaking and unspoken to until I found Ted Fonic, the only human being with whom I felt free to unselfconsciously discuss the things that puzzled and fascinated me.

Mr. Fonic's green eyes lit up at my log. It was as thorough, he said, as it was passionate. Everything I documented with my compass, my protractor, my ruler, and my log mattered to him. If I measured each segment of the major and minor foraging trails established by *C. pennsylvanicus*, he checked to make sure

I'd computed the angles in relation to the starting point. If I counted the number of worker ants making the trip during an hour of observation, he compared one day's count to the next. Did foraging ants use visual cues like sticks or stones to establish their routes? He wanted to know the answer as much as I did. I'd seen pairs of ants moving in tandem, the leader stopping to waggle its rear, the follower taking note, then duplicating the route. Did they tutor each other, demonstrating the path one-on-one? I'd seen a lone, lost carpenter happen upon an empty foraging trail only to swerve onto it and follow it to the destination as clearly as if there'd been a green interstate sign indicating an on-ramp. Had it stumbled upon a chemical track embedded in the ground? If I had a question, Mr. Fonic had it too. I expressed frustration that instead of a simple answer, our observations spawned new questions. Mr. Fonic was pleased with me. "Spoken," he said, "like a true scientist."

V

It was the kind of fall afternoon that
wanted to be two things at once. The wind shook the leaves
of our tree mightily one minute, then died down to nothing
the next. The sun would dart behind a cloud, then shake free
and stand exposed. I was sitting on the railroad bank smoking a cigarette, sorely tempted to revive my old tradition of
producing accomplishments in the reeds, when I heard familiar bicycle tires. Jump Wicket came riding his bike down the
shore road with a magazine tucked under one arm. I madly
crushed out my butt and waved the smoke away. I watched,
transfixed, as he threw his bike down in the reeds like he used
to, then opened up the magazine to the page he liked and flattened it on top of Little Duck's overturned rowboat. He gazed
at it until he was sufficiently excited, then unbuckled his pants,
let them drop to his ankles, and gave it his all. He got a good,
quiet rhythm going. I stuffed my fist in my mouth to keep from
laughing at the look on his face—pleasure made comic by con-
certed effort.

The consummation brought him to his knees. Without sen-
timent, he tossed the magazine under the boat for next time,

jumped on his bike, and rode away. There were dozens of places around Lake Mary for privacy. Why did Jump return to the reeds? Did he miss molesting blind, retarded, deformed little me? Without demanding proof or testimony, without subjecting the hypothesis to the rigors of testing, something quivering and craven inside me decided to believe this was so. I ran down to the boat to study the magazine.

Sexy photographs of near-naked Playmates making fools of themselves filled page after page. At home in my pink bedroom, I stood in front of the full-length mirror. I took off my clothes. From head to toe I was clean. My ribs no longer jutted out painfully against the skin. My belly was smooth. I was well built and well fed. I tried out the poses. Standing with legs spread, hands on hips, brazen, coy, prepared to be cruel. Sprawling in relative modesty across my pink carpet, wearing only the top to my baby-doll pajamas, my lips puckered, my eyes kittenish, cowering, easily hurt, the picture of chastity except for one tentative finger lightly stroking my vagina. Squatting with bossy bravado, flashing the mirror a major beaver shot while pinching my own nipples erect and licking my top lip with the tip of my tongue. This last one was the most difficult pose to sustain. I could never hold it for very long without falling over backward. Practice was needed. The spine of the magazine was broken so that it fell open to this page. Clearly this was Jump's favorite pose. Afterward, I kissed myself in the mirror to see where my nose would go when the real thing happened.

In the name of science, I waited for Jump every day after school, smoking myself sick on the railroad bank in between trips down to the grass to map the trails. Jump had no set routine. I never knew when he might wend his way to the reeds, throw down his bike, and reach under the boat for the magazine. He might come three days in a row one week, then skip a week or even two. As part of my research, I would verify the precise location of the magazine under the boat each afternoon when I arrived. Had he been there yet or not?

One night, Ollie opened the door to my bedroom and caught me squatting naked, thighs spread in front of the mirror, pinching my nipples while concentrating on getting the tippy-tip of my tongue to lick my upper lip like the girl in the magazine. "Princess!" Ollie said, causing me to topple over backward. "What in hell has got into you?"

A lie so preposterous as to be totally convincing sprang to mind. "Darn it all, Ollie," I said. "Now I have to start over. I heard on the bus that if a girl squats naked half an hour a day she'll have shorter periods."

"Princess!" Ollie said. "That is the biggest load of horseshit I ever heard. Sit down on the bed. Ollie will tell you the facts of life." It was difficult to keep a straight face. Ollie waded through euphemisms for every body part and purpose, portraying intercourse in the most misty, abstract, uninformative terms as something gentle that went on under the sheets in the dark behind closed doors when a man and a woman really loved each other and wanted to spend their lives together and could afford to buy a house, which meant they were ready to have a baby. Then, we gals were grateful that when God made us, he filled us with little eggs.

—

At Bridge Night, Ollie learned about the monthly mixers
sponsored by Methodist Youth Fellowship. I agreed to attend.
Ollie drove me to the church basement, then sat on one of
the folding chairs lined up in a row against the wall for the
chaperones. We teens drank Hawaiian Punch out of Dixie
cups. The braver ones offered chaste versions of rock and roll
dancing. Ollie's eyes were bright with bitterness even in the
darkness as she watched our next-door neighbor, good-looking, athletic Stevie Paludy, ask everyone to dance but me. It
took all the restraint she could muster not to hump over there
and demand that he ask me too. In a church basement, of all
places, someone ought to be Christian enough to rescue a girl
from spending the evening as a wallflower. Well, the wrong
someone was.

Calhoun Hayes, Abraham Lincoln's other science nerd, was
motivated by the irresistible bass line of "Green Onions" by
Booker T and the MGs to stop picking calcified boogers out of
the upper recesses of his nose and cross the floor to me. Ollie
was mortified as Calhoun pulled me out onto the waxed linoleum. Neither of us knew how to dance. We thrashed our forearms up and down, shifting our weight with great momentum
back and forth like hobbyhorses. Emphatic feverish fascination
filled Calhoun's eyes. To voice attraction, he described the prin-
ciple of resistance in electricity.

Next, they played a slow dance, "It's All in the Game." Ollie's
mouth fell open in a horrified grimace as Calhoun remained
on the dance floor, less to dance than to complete his diatribe
on resistance. Before any further social damage could be done,
Ollie crossed the linoleum, grabbed my hand, and led me out.
"Never dance twice with a dork," she said in the dark on the

way to the car. "People will think you're going steady."

"I'm sorry, Ollie," I said.

"Don't you worry, Princess," Ollie said, accidentally revealing the unreassuring gravity of the situation as she understood it. "Ollie will find you a beau if it kills her."

—

Winter was coming. *C. pennsylvanicus* stepped up foraging activities down at the pharmacist's house. I ran back and forth to the log, manic with purpose, counting madly, notating trails schematically on graph paper to within one-sixteenth of an inch. On the night of the first frost, as if they'd checked the date in the *Farmer's Almanac*, they withdrew to spend the winter in the nest. They had stored enough food and water to get through until spring. Jump hibernated too.

Students crowded around the terrarium all winter to laugh at the tedious, futile activities of *C. pennsylvanicus*. Some ants went around in circles. Others climbed up the glass wall of the terrarium to the rim and let themselves slide helplessly back down. I tried to keep the terrarium sequestered and dark, with plenty of air, neither too hot nor too cold. But the larvae looked dry. The worker ants were feeding only themselves. They weren't tending the larvae the way they should. A few loyal workers stayed near the queen, forming an entourage around her. They brought her agar goo and tried to feed her mouth-to-mouth. Sometimes she ate. Other times she just turned away. They licked her body with their tongues. I hoped the antibiotic in their special gland was still working.

—

In spring, Ollie and I shopped for Easter suits sewn of linen in delicate pastels, their style a nod to Jacqueline Kennedy. Our new purses matched our shoes. Our gloves were white. It wasn't men we hoped to attract with these chaste, upwardly mobile getups, but the mothers of men. We hoped the female congregants at the Methodist church would say to their sons over Easter ham, "Didn't that Hopkins gal look lovely in church today? Why don't you take *her* to the movies?" Nothing.

Jump was back with a new magazine. I watched from the railroad bank as he gave it his all. He rode his bike back down the shore road and I skidded down the slope to the grass to admire the ants. *C. pennsylvanicus* had multiplied and divided impressively. The colony was well on its way to maturity. By contrast, the carpenters in the terrarium were listless. They were unhappy. Their numbers were greatly reduced. They weren't boring new tunnels or chambers. They weren't disposing of their dead. Perhaps they missed their old expeditions out in the light and air of the world for hours at a time, looking for oranges and honey. Mr. Fonic asked our friends at ISU for advice. They suggested we motivate the workers by creating a foraging zone, placing an empty milk bottle at one end of the terrarium and baiting it inside with a proven treat. We chose an orange. They perked up.

For summer, Ollie and I chose new Lycra swimsuits in avocado green splashed with orange poppies. The plunging neckline would allow the boys of Lake Mary to see for themselves what the lovely Hopkins gal had to offer. We rolled our chaises out onto the front lawn into the sun to work on our tans. We waded in Lake Mary, tossing a large, inflated beach ball coyly back and forth to each other to attract male attention. Nothing.

We worked on our hair. Ollie gave up her flip. I gave up my bob. We both got beehives. She sat me down at the kitchen table and trimmed my bangs. She ratted the hair on the crown of my head, then combed a layer of long hair over the ratty mound. She pinned it in place, spraying my whole head with hair spray until it felt as if it were made of wood. Her turn. She sat down and I did a wobbly version of the same thing to her. The September *Vogue* arrived in August. Ollie studied page after page, choosing our new look for fall. We drove to Diamond's in our beehives to shop for the collegiate look, tailored wool blazers and pleated, plaid Pendleton skirts. Ollie watched with smitten eyes as I boarded the bus for the first day of school.

A year of captivity had gone by. The orange peels in the foraging bottle were developing a microscopic mold. Either our captive ants had stopped rubbing their antibiotic on each other or it was no longer working. More ants died. "Don't take it so hard," Mr. Fonic said to me the day we found the queen belly-up, but I was inconsolable. *Camponotus* queens were supposed to live for eighteen to twenty-nine years. We'd been selfish and cruel. We'd removed living things from their happy native environment and forced them to struggle in an unhappy artificial one. Instead of returning them to the wild when things didn't work out, we continued experimenting with them until they died. We had played God with them the way God sometimes played God with us. We hadn't done unto others whatsoever we would that others should do unto us. The entomologists warned me. This was just the beginning. In all scientific experiment, the ends justified the means. It was another way of saying that a life in science was going to be one big breaking of the Golden Rule.

—

Nuptial queens lived longer in lab situations than queens taken from nature because nuptial queens were much less sensitive to light. They hadn't spent their lives stuck down in their dark nests all day making egg after egg—only to be dug up and hauled off to a room in an old public school building that was drafty one minute, stale and overheated the next, to be gawked at—tortured, even, I discovered—by cruel adolescents. Mr. Fonic and I agreed to try the ant farm again—this time with virgin ant queens.

—

On warm days in late spring, the virgin ant queen feels the compulsion to mate. She unfolds her lovely, never-used wings and flies away from the nest where she was born and raised, leaving her mother, the queen of the colony, behind. She is also leaving behind her sisters. They are either virgin reproductives like herself, or they have been sterilized to become workers. If necessary, to ensure success, carpenter workers help synchronize nuptial flights. If a virgin queen attempts to fly away to mate too early, she is physically dragged back into the nest entrance by workers. The sight of the nuptial queen taking flight excites male ants who also have wings. The scent emitted by the queen is so pleasant, it drives them wild. Sometimes it is strong enough to be smelled by humans. The males take flight, pursuing the nuptial queen.

Male ants have sperm. They are born with all the sperm inside they will ever possess. In preparation for the moment of mating, the male's sperm is transferred from follicles to the seminal vesicles, where it is primed for ejaculation. The male ant approaches the queen, stroking her with his antennae. He gets behind her, grasping her by the thorax, and attempts to insert his copulatory organs into her cloaca. Once he succeeds, he discharges most of his sperm along with mucus. In species where queens are intended to produce huge broods, one male cannot supply all of the sperm she will need. A second male approaches and grasps her thorax—and, sometimes, a third.

After mating, male ants have fulfilled their single purpose on earth. They conveniently die. The queen tears off her wings for she will fly no more. She finds an agreeable site and builds a nest. She will rear the first brood of workers alone, drawing on her own reserves to produce eggs, as well as to keep herself alive and well.

—

We'd had a lovely soft rain. The sky was clearing in the west. Conditions were perfect. I walked down the railroad tracks, armed with an array of large-mouthed Mason jars with holes punched into the lids. I hovered at the ready, awaiting the annual frolic: winged queens mating with winged lovers on the wing. Here they came. It was too lovely. It was too free. It was not something that belonged in a jar, but it was a means to an end. I caught three.

Black curtains cordoned off all three terrariums now, controlling the level of darkness and keeping out the draft. All of our queens were productive. I watched them lay egg after egg that summer, as if they didn't know they were indoors. The eggs became plump, viable larvae, evolving slowly into pupae with soft, white cocoons. I kept my fingers crossed, curious as to why I permitted myself a superstitious gesture regarding the outcome of a scientific experiment.

—

Hair spray gave mice cancer. I showed the abstract to Ollie. Ollie threw ours in the garbage. We laboriously took turns combing out the ratting from our beehives once and for all, saying, *Ouch, ouch, ouch,* all afternoon. We bought a blow-dryer. We shampooed me, we blew me dry, we styled my hair softly turned under. We feathered my bangs, keeping them so long they grazed my eyelashes. "Twirl your hair," Ollie said and I turned my head in slow motion right-left-right like the girl did on TV to show how soft and swingy Prell made her hair. Old-fashioned femininity was in this fall. We bought high-collared blouses with ruffles down the front. Our skirts were calf-length dirndls. Our knee-high leather boots sported a medium heel.

At Bridge Night, Ollie learned about cheerleading tryouts. She signed me up. I wanted to cooperate with Ollie. I practiced every night in the living room, yelling at Ollie, who sat on the sofa yelling back at me, playing the role of the entire student body. I stood before her with my legs stiff and straight, three feet apart, hands on hips. With an exaggerated athleticism, I mimed the gesture for speaking loud to the hard-of-hearing, placing the flats of my open hands parallel at either side of my mouth to yell, "Give me an L!" I clapped twice.

"L!" she yelled.

"Give me an I!" Clap-clap.

"I!"

"Give me an N!" Clap-clap.

"N!"

"Give me a C!" Clap-clap.

"C!"

"Give me an O!" Clap-clap.

"O!"

"Give me another L!" I yelled, sending Ray into soundless hysterics so bad Ollie made him leave the room.

Ollie was ecstatic when I told her the three judges had called me back to repeat my audition solo. I didn't tell her it was so they could have a good laugh. Ollie and I had practiced the cheers exactly wrong, producing two claps where there was supposed to be a beat of silence and silence where there were supposed to be claps. One after the other, the lips of the poor judges crinkled, quivered, and buckled with snickers—just like Ray's, only worse—as I completed my performance. I was eliminated. Ollie was despondent. She was concerned about my emotional balance. All I cared about was ants.

—

I was despised. I reprimanded any students who left the lights on in the science room, or, worse yet, who opened the window. Scientific experimentation required strict control. My efforts were rewarded. A very high percentage of pupae hatched, resulting in our first successful indoor brood. Dozens of new daughters selflessly divided the tasks, some building new tunnels and chambers, others striking out along our phony foraging trails for arbitrarily placed oranges and honey. The workers who tended the queen made the short trip to the agar goo dish, bringing it back to feed her mouth-to-mouth. In return, she stroked them with her antennae as she should, providing them with God-knows-what in the way of chemicals. One of the ISU boys hypothesized that what was being transferred was a chemical that contained colony odor, odor that would allow colony members to recognize each other as kin.

Only science-minded students were allowed to gather around the terrariums now. Idle torturers were asked to leave. Those who stayed were impressed by the industriousness of ants. They commented on the absence of confusion, duplication, or laziness. They lost their prejudice, no longer seeing ants as only household pests. One of these was Jump.

He spent his lunch hour hovering over the terrariums, just as I did. There was light rage in his chin. His eyes were vacant, but something about the cold, efficient, pathetic success of ants engaged his deeper attention. I flirted like a nerd, holding forth on the sophistication of ants compared to us in a voice made musical by infatuation. I explained that in the wild, *C. pennsylvanicus* possessed an aptitude for math as acute as its willingness to cooperate. My computations of the segments along the Tanner Trail showed they had a marked preference for the angle of sixty degrees. Nothing ants did was arbitrary. Sixty degrees had to be an angle of proven survival, an angle that either aided trail formation, prevented directional errors, foiled predators, or accomplished all three at once. Based on this and other mystifying unities, I explained to Jump, Mr. Fonic and I had calculated that the carpenter ants on the Tanner Trail were all using the same algorithm.

Mr. Fonic had never seen this side of me. He stood behind his desk, his shoulders loose in their supple jacket, his long hands flexed, his lips slack, his head lightly cocked to one side as I invited Jump to come to the pharmacist's house to see the marvels of *C. pennsylvanicus* at work in the wild for himself. There was a hint of man-to-man appreciation in Ted Fonic's green eyes, a complex pleasure in the set of his lips. I'd never seen this side of him before either. Perhaps he had a soft spot for white-trash sadists too.

—

Our desperate search for social exposure for me took us back to Methodist Youth Fellowship. There was a new crop of awkward, disoriented, self-conscious social misfits looking for fellowship in the basement of the Methodist church, yet Calhoun Hayes was right where we'd left him, lurking along the sidelines with his finger in the upper recesses of his nose, as if waiting for me to return for the next dance. With an air of defeat, Ollie settled into a folding chair along the wall with the other chaperones and watched us thrash.

—

One day, a letter arrived at our ranch house from the convent. "What did Sister Anne have to say for herself?" I piped up at the supper table. After nearly three years with Ollie and Ray, I knew how to chat about this and that over the evening meal.

"Oh!" Ollie said as if I'd stepped on her foot. She looked at Ray, not me, to answer. "She wrote. To say. She's so glad. You're—doing fine!"

I looked over at Ray too, to see why we should. Ray's eyes scanned the real me gently for the first time, as if I were a girl in a crowd he had to identify and drive somewhere far, far away. Ollie wasn't smiling. Her eyes were sad. Something compelled me to speak frankly. "Academically, maybe," I said. "But I'm not doing fine socially. Princess knows Ollie is disappointed in her."

I would never speak frankly again. Something in my tone caused Ollie to burst into deep, terrifying sobs. I threw down my spoon and leapt to her side, hugging her to the best of my ability while she remained seated in the chair with her head in her hands.

Ray patted his lips lightly with a napkin and stood up.

"Thank you," Ray said to Ollie as she sobbed. "That was good." He went for a drive. He had barely touched his food.

—

The mortality of colony-founding queens was extremely high, even in nature. Just because *Camponotus* queens *could* live eighteen to twenty-nine years didn't mean they did. If the queen survived the precarious period during which she reared the first worker brood, the colony sometimes ran into trouble in the second delicate phase between the first brood and the second. In the classroom, of course, the percentages were worse. It was touch and go. Our three terrariums were clean. Our temperatures were consistent, our light levels low. The large, open foraging zones we offered had attracted workers at first. The long, jazzy lines they'd initially formed to get to the assorted food sources mimicked what I saw in the field. But now, two of the three captive branches of *C. pennsylvanicus* were in decline. The workers were weak, overcoming inertia, depression, or the flu, stumbling along the trail like drunks. The queens had stopped laying eggs.

There was only a handful of microbes that were deadly to ants. One, a fungus, had been associated with *C. pennsylvanicus* since 1891. It situated itself in the abdominal segments, ultimately covering the host in a toxic white mass. I examined our workers with a magnifying glass, fearing for the worst, but finding nothing.

—

Ollie and I bowed our heads in church on Easter Sunday, banging brims. We accidentally looked comical. Our huge white straw hats had appeared stately in the mirror at the hat counter at Diamond's, but they were too floppy for the purposes of the Methodist pews. *Please, please, please, God*, I prayed, *don't let the last queen die.* In the science room, we were down to one queen and a handful of workers. I was fully aware that I was praying selfishly to get my way. I wanted my little wish on record so it could compete with all the little wishes of everyone else in the world, as if prayer were no more exalted than superstition. All that talk about *Not my will but thine be done*—that was a lot of guff. *Let my will be done*—that was what prayer was about.

"Amen," everyone in the congregation said aloud. To help my case, I kept my head bowed. *Please, please, please, God*, I prayed, as if it were my queen ant on the cross, not Christ, *let her live.*

—

For the second time, a sex scandal concerning one of the Paludy boys shook Lake Mary. First, it had been Mark, the oldest Paludy, who got his steady girlfriend pregnant in their senior year. They married soon after graduation and she could rapidly be seen in maternity clothes, pausing in the cake mix aisle of the supermarket, while he stood with his hands in his pockets in the showroom of the Cadillac dealership, befuddled at his instant maturity. Now it was Jimmy, the middle Paludy. Poor Donna Stark. They'd only gone steady for a month. Jimmy claimed he'd never touched her. Now, instead of donning a mortarboard and a commencement gown, off she went to St. Vincent's Home for Unwed Mothers in Dubuque. She was a pregnant teenage dropout, the worst thing an Iowa girl could be. "I Was a Pregnant Teenage Dropout," read the title of the cover story in *Teen Magazine* on the rack in the drugstore. Donna Stark would never see her baby. It would be given up for adoption.

"Princess!"

"Yes, Ollie."

"Does Stevie Paludy ever make passes at you?"

"No, Ollie."

"Good," she said. "The way Grace Paludy snubs us, I don't want no rubber-bustin' bastard of hers trying to get in Daughter's pants."

My face was contorted with an ardent grimace. The rubber-bustin' bastard who had gotten in Daughter's pants was Jump.

—

I had recently succumbed to the pull of my old love. These days when I walked down the railroad tracks with my tools and my log, Jump would already be there, waiting for me on the railroad bank. On his face was a temporary docility forged by lust. We'd share a cigarette, then he would lie back and look at the sky while I measured, counted, and compared the trails of *C. pennsylvanicus*, entering the results in the log.

Sometimes Jump and I would walk down to the reeds. Other times we'd retreat to the sheltered area under the railroad transom. When it rained, we slipped inside and settled ourselves in one of the sad, moldy rooms of my father's house. With no fear of exposure I took off my clothes. This was not the same body Jump had messed with so long ago. My deformity still hovered beneath my bangs, but he didn't go anywhere near it.

Once a sadist, always a sadist. Jump would keep going when I asked him to stop. He would pin my arms back to the point where they hurt instead of stopping at the point where restraint was still exciting. There was one thing he demanded that I refused. It was the thing he used to make me do. I was afraid I'd do it the same way now that I used to do then. Even without that kind of proof to expose me, something about me would sometimes bother him. With his eyes on mine, he would get a troubling association. Behind my horn-rims, I waited him out. He wasn't bright enough to track his thought sequence. Whatever nagged at him, he brushed aside. He hurt me, he defied me. But I didn't care, as long as he didn't recognize me.

—

Our queen made it. Her first brood of workers was still in loyal attendance. Drowsy and lacking in confidence, they still managed to feed her regurgitated food as they were programmed to do, while she stroked them over and over with her antennae. I watched breathlessly as she wended her way back down to her special chamber. She was laying new eggs right on time.

—

Ollie and I had a fight. Every summer, the Arnold Community Players performed a musical to the best of their ability on the stage of the town hall. Ollie had always wanted to see Daughter onstage. This year, they were doing *The Music Man*. *The Music Man* was written by an Iowan and set in Mason City, Ollie's hometown. There was a part that was perfect for me—Marian the Librarian. Ollie's favorite song was Marian's great hit, "Till There Was You." For several weeks leading up to the auditions, the Players were offering free group lessons from a noted voice coach. Ollie wanted me to attend.

I refused. Ollie was grating on my nerves. I knew I couldn't sing. I hadn't gotten my real mother's gorgeous voice. I was tired of being humiliated in public due to Ollie's unrealistic hopes for me, though the recurring situations were a constant moral reminder of what it felt like to be experimented on. What I wanted was for Ollie to drive me to school every day so I could do something I was good at. I wanted to hover over, nurse, and tend our magnificent, brave, exhausted queen as she nurtured the second fragile worker brood.

Ollie's features grew belligerent. "Darn it all, Princess," she said. "Pretty soon, you'll be all grown up and stuck in some laboratory running experiments night and day. Then you'll realize you missed every good thing about being young." Her voice was forlorn. I understood. She meant *she* was missing every good thing about me being young. I compromised. I would audition, but *she* would coach me in the car on the way to school. She went for it.

"There were bells," we sang together in the car, "on the hill, But I never heard them ringing, No, I never heard them at all, Till there was you." I tried rehearsing solo in the science room. My voice reverberated against the granite floors. Not only did it sound professional, the ants seemed to like it. Now I threw my heart and soul into the words, fully aware that these very words just moments ago had seemed unbearably bland and sentimental.

The day of the audition, Ollie sat in the audience, mouthing the words along with me, her eyes proud and confident. I stood onstage, sweeping my arm through the air with all the grace of a windmill, then woodenly clutching my bosom to bellow, "And there was music, And there were wonderful roses, They tell me." To keep from laughing, the director had to press his two lips together until they disappeared entirely inside the cavity of his mouth. I was eliminated.

Ollie fumed about the casting inequity all summer. When she and Ray went to the play, she came home outraged. "The girl they picked sang just as flat as you, Princess," she said. She wasn't herself again until August. *Vogue* arrived.

Horn-rims were out. Wire rims were in. I wore my hair like Peggy, the girl on *The Mod Squad*, long and straight, parted loosely in the middle. A flicker of my deformity was visible in the middle of my forehead. Peggy and I both lived with the same secret from our past. Her mother was a prostitute in San Francisco, California, mine in Arnold, Iowa. At Diamond's, Ollie and I took the escalator past Separates and headed straight for the Mod Shop. We bought me low-cut, stretchy tops that snapped like baby clothes at the crotch. These were paired with hip-hugging miniskirts. Ollie's eyes grew moist at the sight of me. "Daughter," she said, "this is the year you knock them dead."

The skies of Iowa were never bluer than in the early days of September. The clouds were never whiter. The afternoon sun was warm on my arms after a sweet, soaking rain. I dreamed of recombination. If the indoor civilization stabilized, we could try returning half the ants to their relatives in the original, outdoor colony. Would they recognize each other as kin? Would the colony odor produced in the terrarium with all this stroking of antennae be familiar to both groups? Would they know they were long-lost sisters? If so, we could expect to see an absence of aggression, a reaction of casual tolerance, a huddling together, followed by the exchange of food.

But what if the odor of the terrarium workers differed significantly? They might be treated as foreigners. If so, there was a continuum of aggressive behaviors we could expect. Low on the aggression scale would be avoidance. A little higher was intense antennation with open jaws. Still higher, a spitting fight. I would have considered a spitting fight a setback, even though I was dying to see ants furiously tossing regurgitated liquids at each other. More aggressive than a spitting fight was intimidating posturing. *Camponotus* would stand their ground with stiffened legs and repeatedly, rapidly jerk their bodies forward and backward, their jaws wide open. Further provocation would cause them to seize the intruder and drag it away. The final hostility level involved a full, coordinated attack, concluding with biting the foreigner to death. We hoped to see none of this.

Mr. Fonic and I agreed. If these eggs made it to the adult worker stage, we would attempt recombination. Whichever way the experiment went, toward recognition and mutual respect, or toward total destruction of half of the clan, we would observe the results over a three-month period and offer quantitative analysis of what we'd seen. Our experiment was sure to win the Westinghouse National High School Science Competition.

—

Ollie was casting her net wider. In her large, round, halting handwriting, she compiled a list of blind dates for me, mining organizations other than Bridge Night, from the League of Women Voters to the Republican Party. We were looking for males from distant schools, neighborhoods, and churches, males who hadn't heard of or met us before, who didn't know Princess was an antisocial nerd too smart for her own good. Ollie went down the list, calling the mothers of the youths in question to arrange a meeting place, setting a day, planning my outfit, then driving me to the designated place—the ice cream shop, the movie theater, the pizza parlor—and waiting in the car for me while the boy never showed. "People around here have got no manners whatsoever," Ollie would say by way of explanation every time. "And they think *we're* coarse." She refused to see what was plain to me. Some no-shows were no-goes. A car would pull up. The boy would take one look and dive to the floor, urging his parent to gun it.

—

Our indoor workers were flourishing. They had made it through the winter months with no casualties. Instead of fussing over them, Mr. Fonic and I had been able to spend the time studying abstracts detailing the pitfalls other scientists had encountered in recombination experiments. We read them aloud to each other, making notes, planning for the big day.

Conditions at the site were key. Ted Fonic himself drove out to the pharmacist's house in his sports car, a teal blue 1957 Ford Thunderbird. It was a cold spring day. The wind was testy. When a cloud raced across the sun, we shivered. We walked the length and breadth of the colony network, weighing the advantages and disadvantages of every potential recombination site. We rejected both the main headquarters and the infestation in the windowsill. The most remote outpost—that was the safest bet. It was moister there and shadier. We were standing side by side under the tree, watching the surface of Lake Mary bulge languidly in slow billows. A wave of immeasurable emotion unaccounted for in all my log entries swept up my spine. I'd read about the amygdala, the almond-shaped mass of nuclei deep in the temporal lobe. It was the seat of the emotional responses and hormonal secretions that controlled autonomic responses associated with fear. I had assumed I was missing one. Apparently not. I thought I might faint. I had to sit down and lean back against the trunk of the tree.

Mr. Fonic looked down at me with level green eyes. An explanation was in order. "This," I said, "means a lot to me."

—

We were ready. The sun was shining. The air was warm and moist. We risked it. We mixed nests. I walked down the railroad tracks with a jar containing my biggest, most beautiful terrarium queen and half her workers. They hated being jostled. They froze in place. I set the jar down on its side three feet away from the ideal outpost. I took off the lid and sat down to watch. The terrarium workers were smaller and lighter in color. They were scared. They reared up on their hind legs to feel this new thing—real air. They ventured out onto new soil a few paces, antennating each other as if to remind themselves who they were. They paused as if waiting for their surroundings to tell them what to do. The queen alone never budged. She stayed hidden deep in the soil of the jar, storing up her energy for the ordeals to come. Just a few yards away, the outdoor workers blithely continued their tasks.

An outdoor scout picked up their scent. The scout sent out a chemical announcement to convey possible territorial encroachment. Other scouts veered away from their customary rounds and joined in what appeared to be a casual, exploratory border check. The indoor ants smelled the scouts coming. Some huddled together. Others tried to flee to their deeper, darker chambers, forgetting they were no longer in the terrarium in the classroom.

Intense antennation occurred between the outdoor scouts and the indoor workers. One scout broke away, forging brazenly into the jar to meet the queen. How proud I was of her. She somehow projected majesty. The scout responded accordingly, reacting with deference. Their meeting went on for a while. The scout exited, sending out a signal, *A-OK*. The outdoor ants went back to work. A few indoor workers tagged along. Crossing the outpost borders, the indoor ants were intrigued, picking up a riot of fascinating scent trails laid down by their relatives. Were they welcome?

There was a brief skirmish. A few point women were bitten to death and lugged away bodily to be stored as food. I held my breath. There was a period of intense antennation with open jaws, but no spitting fight. No further casualties were suffered. Order prevailed. The indoor ants were permitted to join the march to the food. Day one: Success!

—

Within a matter of weeks, the terrarium workers lost their light color, growing almost as dark and glossy as their cousins in the field. They were putting on weight. Distinguishing the respective clan members became difficult. I did the best I could to quantify the integration process, but my log showed I was losing track. I thought everyone was getting along. One afternoon, in broad daylight, a field queen walked over and killed my terrarium queen. It took eight field workers to drag her large, lovely body away. I swallowed hard. I had caught that queen on her virgin nuptial flight. It was bittersweet, but in ninety days, we had a full-fledged reunion. I wrote it up. We submitted our findings to Westinghouse, meeting the October 15 deadline.

—

Ollie found a new approach for socializing me: older men. College students had their own cars and enough spending money to take Daughter out to dinner. Ollie extracted random names from the boys at ISU. She called them first to introduce the concept of a gal too intellectually mature for high school boys, then made them call back to ask me for a date. I set the day and the time. I chose the place. The doorbell *did* ring. We answered it. Success! A male was standing before us like he said he would.

At some point in the transaction, we'd given the wrong signal. The college students were looking for sex. When they didn't get it, they didn't call back. "At least you're in circulation," Ollie said. "That will make others sit up and take notice."

One night, the male standing before us looked to be thirty years old, not twenty. There were deep blue bags under his eyes. His skin was yellow. He wore his hair in a crew cut—everyone else these days wore theirs below the ears, if not all the way to the shoulders. He wore a sharkskin suit and a narrow tie. He had said he was a business student at Arnold Community College, but he looked like someone who'd been fired from the FBI. I had a bad feeling about this night. Off we went in his Buick Capri.

I returned just before midnight. I'd walked all the way home from downtown after jumping out of the car while he tried to rape me. Ollie was waiting up, reading a Reader's Digest condensed novel by the light of our floor lamp. "How'd it go?" she said with a yawn when I walked in.

"Not well," I said. I sat down beside her with my dress on backward, a black eye, and one shoe.

"Princess!" Ollie sobbed, leaning over to hug me while I stared at the living room wall. "I'd like to castrate that lying, psycho bastard," she said when her sobbing subsided, grabbing a handful of air in a threatening manner as if it were the pearl handle of a very sharp knife. She wanted revenge. "Ray!" she yelled, waking the poor man up out of a Korean War nightmare.

I sat in the passenger seat of the Plymouth as Ray combed the streets of town, looking in every driveway and alley, in the parking lot of every bar and dorm for a light blue 1963 Buick Capri. The silky, inky darkness of night flowed over our windshield as we prowled the empty streets. Yellow pools of light from the street lamps illuminated municipal mundanities—manhole covers, fire hydrants, mailboxes—rendering them touchingly beautiful. Ray had pulled on his plaid wool hunting jacket over his pajamas. He was still wearing bedroom slippers. On the seat between us was a loaded semiautomatic handgun, a Colt M1911 along with an extra .45 cartridge. I never felt more protected in my entire life. I told him so. He looked at me distantly. "That," he said, "is a God damn shame."

When they closed their bedroom door that night, I eavesdropped. "I can tell you one thing," Ray said to Ollie. "He ain't from here. If he was from here, I'd a found him. I hope you've learned your lesson. Stop meddling and leave that little girl to her science."

—

All winter when I boarded the school bus in the morning and walked down the aisle to my seat in the back, I had to pass both Jump and Cooper Tanner, sitting with their girlfriends. Cooper's was Chrissy Chrisman, the Gidget type with big blue eyes, a little pug nose, and a long, blonde ponytail. Cooper himself was a heartthrob now. His head was still lovely and large. His brown eyes with their long lashes were still prone to daydreams, but daydreams of romance, not landscape architecture. They sat side by side on the bus, holding hands. They were cute together in a juvenile, squishy way that made you want to pinch them hard and say, "It's not real love, what you're feeling."

Jump's girlfriend was Sandy Flood, the famous slut. They necked on the bus. After school, they snuck into the janitor's closet. Everyone could hear them going at it.

—

The issue of queen loyalty gnawed at me. I read every abstract I could get my hands on. Queen ants of some species had been known to eat the eggs of their competitors. Other species of queens bullied and nudged competing queens into having nervous breakdowns or miscarriages. It wasn't completely clear whether a queen decided to be queen or workers elected her by sterilizing everyone else. As in every other survival issue, the fire ants, *Solenopsis invicta*, took queen selection the furthest. When queenless fire-ant workers were introduced to a choice of queens, they executed all but one. Either someone in the species had one heck of a plan for a dynasty, or they all did.

—

A formal letter arrived on Ted Fonic's desk. We won the award. First prize was $40,000 toward college tuition. He was happy. I felt like a fraud. Certain older workers who had been born and raised in the terrarium and remained there as the control group in the recombination experiment were now terminal. I found the telltale white fungus in their abdominal segments. One was already covered in a deadly white mass. Had removing half the indoor colony upset the chemical balance, allowing microbial predators an edge? I was frustrated. There was a vast, diverse, complex, invisible universe to study, bigger exponentially than our visible universe, but it could only be seen under a microscope. Abraham Lincoln High School didn't have one strong enough. I read what I could.

—

Microbes were smart. They lived in communities called biofilms. Talk about effective group communication—they could emit a signal telling millions where to settle down and raise a family of more millions. Microbes survived by sensing changes in the environment deleterious to a healthy lifestyle. Clostridium, for example. When a clostridium living in the soil got the feeling that home was about to become unsafe, that food was about to get scarce, that water was about to run out, or that the climate was about to become too hot to survive, that clostridium knew how to save her entire species. She made a daughter cell, copying her chromosome inside herself. She wrapped it in a bunting made of cell fluid, forming a membrane. She wrapped again, forming a second membrane, then coated the whole little double-wrapped daughter cell with a layer of proteins and nutrients so hard the daughter could survive for up to 250 million years. The mother cell then withered away, destroyed by the disasters she knew were imminent. The daughter lay dormant, enduring all, waiting until things were better. She could tell. When that day dawned, when the air was sweet and cool and the food was back and the water was plentiful again, the little spore transformed herself back into a cell, bringing her entire kind to life again.

Microbes were not only smart, they were fast. A single bacterium dividing once an hour became the progenitor of 281 trillion cells in forty-eight hours. There were good microbes and bad. Good microbes could be used to treat all kinds of disorders, to boost immune systems, to soothe stomachs upset by certain antibiotics, to help with colitis and bowel cancer. Bad microbes had shaped history. Among the most notorious was *Yersinia pestis*, the bubonic plague, also known as the Black Death. A quarter of the population of Europe—including half the population of London—was destroyed in seven years, as *Yersinia pestis* was carried from one infected rat to another by fleas—and through casual, incidental contact, to humans.

Almost as bad was *Phytophthora infestans*. In nineteenth-century Ireland, *P. infestans* destroyed the potato crops, causing poverty, homelessness, and famine. The potato plant had no natural ability to fight off *P. infestans*. The fungus spread like wildfire across the entire country. Some of the Irish blamed the rotting of the crops on "the little people," the fairies that lived in special, very great, old fairy trees. Others believed it was the work of the devil. They made retribution by sprinkling the fields with holy water to drive away demons. Those of a less religious bent blamed electricity. A new form of transportation was ruining the land—trains. As they went chugging across the land, trains discharged electricity into the air, causing the blight that killed the crops. Before the cause could be identified and a new, resistant strain of potato plant developed, a million Irish starved to death.

—

I lost them all. It was a simple task, emptying the terrarium, disposing of the contents, cleaning and shining the four glass walls. It was easily done even when one was numb. Given the total decimation of the indoor colony, I was grateful to have something concrete, something necessary yet superficial to do.

—

All summer, we'd heard Jump and Sandy Flood going at it in the woods behind his house. So why in September did he come back to me? I would be down at the pharmacist's house, smoking on the railroad bank prior to skidding down the slope to review the cooperation level between the two clans. I would hear his bicycle wheels coming down the shore road. I should have felt flattered. Rumor had it that Sandy Flood would do anything, including that one thing I wouldn't do for Jump for fear he'd recognize me. Why did he still need ugly me?

Something in me was beginning to rebel at the pretense required to live a double daily life. "I Was a Teenage Werewolf," read the title of the cover story in *Teen Magazine* on the rack in the drugstore. I knew the feeling. When Jump would show up at the pharmacist's house, I found myself acting alluring and excitable. I'd go through the motions. The fact was, I was tired of him. I was beginning to dislike our routine and the unvarying way it incorporated his hatred for all women into the specific humiliation and light torture of me. Submission no longer became me. I was relieved if Jump wasn't there. I had resumed my old practice of producing accomplishments in the reeds.

—

Fast and furious, envelopes containing offers of scholarships were arriving in the mail. Dearest to my heart was the one from the boys at ISU. They were not only granting me a full, four-year scholarship to the university, but were guaranteeing me the exalted and much desired work-study role as their lab assistant.

It was Indian summer. The wind was blowing through my hair. The sky was clear. The air was balmy. The humidity was perfect. The sun on my arms felt like a caress. I was sitting under the tree where the shack used to be. A wave of yellow affection came rolling toward me. My sister. How I missed her. Every year when Ollie got our new telephone book, I looked for Cavanaughs. There were none. I was older now than Jima was when I'd last seen her. The county had yanked us out of the shack and driven us over the railroad tracks to town, down to the county building to be placed. Our answer to most of their questions was, *I don't know.*

"Age?"

"I don't know."

"Address?"

"I don't know."

"Age of father?"

"I don't know."

"Whereabouts of father?"

"I don't know."

"Age of mother?"

"I don't know."

"Whereabouts of mother?"

"I don't know."

"Grade last completed in public school?"

That was the only precise answer we could provide. "None."

The people processing us went into another room to call around to find beds for us. We stood together, shivering, our sides completely touching. They came back. I went first. We never dreamed they would be cruel enough to separate us. They led me out of the building. A police car was waiting for me at the curb. Jima and me locked eyes as long as we could, Jima climbing up on a chair to watch through the window that took up the top half of the door, me looking over my shoulder, twisting a full one hundred and eighty degrees until my head looked like it was on backward. I never saw her again.

—

Ollie was losing me to ISU. She worked off her anxiety through weekly trips to Diamond's, excessively and prematurely preparing me for dorm life. In rain, sleet, and snow, she dashed down to Des Moines. My sheets had to match my comforter. I needed a desk lamp with a switch that would accommodate a three-way bulb. I needed shoe bags and padded hangers, a bookcase, a bulletin board. Everything had to be the best. Nothing was too good for Princess. Ollie humped from the car into the living room, dragging purchases for me to admire. I thanked her profusely, trying to sound enthused, offering the kind of mother-daughter commentary she was looking for. One afternoon she came home with an expensive quilted Kleenex box cover. She held it next to my new quilted throw pillow to show me how closely they matched. I was speechless. She burst into tears. "What will I do without you," she said, wiping her eyes.

Ollie needed something new to do. I agreed to go to the senior prom. Ollie had months to work on it and she needed them all. Some mornings when I came into the kitchen for my bowl of Kellogg's Corn Flakes, Ollie would be sitting there in befuddlement with her big tongue in the corner of her mouth, studying the old blind-date list. Lines had been drawn through every boy's name, but there were some she was willing to reconsider. She called a few. No go.

———

A single bacterium dividing once an hour became the progenitor of 281 trillion cells in forty-eight hours. Cell growth of all types followed the law of exponential development. Soon, even a single fertilized human egg had weight and took up space. I knew firsthand. Jump, that rubber-bustin' bastard, had fertilized me. I couldn't tell Ollie.

The prom was exceedingly near. My escort had yet to be found. With my permission, Ollie screwed up her courage to telephone the mother of Calhoun Hayes, who accepted on his behalf. We drove down to Diamond's to canvas Formal Wear for the perfect gown. Ollie found it—a sleek, strapless sheath sewn of pearl-pink satin. "Princess looks puffy," Ollie had said when we had to try on the gown in a larger size. I stood on the step stool in the fitting room at Diamond's sucking in my stomach while the tailor marked the hem of the gown. By prom night, Princess had gotten puffier. The sleek pink satin sheath hitched up in two places, but Ollie's eyes flowed over them both as if they weren't there.

My satin spike heels were dyed pink to match the gown. Accessories included elbow-length white gloves, a simple strand of pearls, and dangly pearl earrings. We did my hair "up." A fountain of waves and curls appeared to fall carelessly from a clasp, though they were in fact pinned rigidly in place. Across my forehead, to cover my deformity, Ollie combed a great swoop of hair. We did my lips and nails. Ollie confiscated my eyeglasses—they ruined the look. When I stood before Ollie in my regal hairdo, strapless and shimmering, my long white gloves rising to the elbow, my pearls at my neck, blind as a bat, her eyes grew moist. If Audrey Hepburn looked like Benjamin Franklin, she'd be a dead ringer for me.

We sat on our sofa together, watching TV, waiting for Calhoun. We watched and waited from 6:00 p.m. until midnight, me with a wide, wincing smile frozen on my face. A glacier had once covered Iowa. How I wished tonight it would return. Ollie sat beside me, weeping. She was blubbering so hard the whole sofa rocked, blowing her nose into a hankie, folding it over and over. I wondered how she could continue to fold it over and still find a dry corner. I hadn't had the courage to mention to Ollie that the week before my identity had been exposed. Everyone in Abraham Lincoln High School knew who I really was. Jump had arrived so late one afternoon that he had surprised me in the reeds, engrossed in the production of Zn, a first. Something about the complacent way I squatted there with my jeans down around my ankles, something about the curious way I could not resist inspecting my accomplishment afterward—something about everything made me, Princess Hopkins, a dead ringer for Crane Cavanaugh.

VI

I was the monster from the scary end of Lake Mary. I was supposed to be institutionalized somewhere with other monsters like me, blind, starved, and deformed. Yet for six years, I had walked down the shore road to the school bus in the morning along with everyone else, breathing the same air breathed by everyone else, getting straight As in every class and scoring 800s on my SATs, winning $40,000 for playing with ants. It was *The Twilight Zone*—right here at Abraham Lincoln High School.

Talk about group communication. Jump told Radley. Radley told everyone. In less than twenty-four hours, thousands of people had shared a single sentence and reacted as one. I was shunned, as before, but now I was uniformly studied. People felt betrayed, yet curious. How had I deceived them? They would grow silent and cross to the other side of the hall if they saw me approaching, as if I were inhuman and it were contagious. Yet they would watch me out of the corners of their eyes until I was out of sight. Calhoun Hayes took a different approach. When he saw me coming, he turned his back and reversed his path, practicing avoidance no matter how far out of his way it took him. In all of Lake Mary, the only two people who didn't know yet were Ollie and Ray.

Sitting on our sofa at midnight in my pink, floor-length sheath, an explanation was in order. "Ollie." My voice came out a hoarse whisper.

Ollie wiped her nose again. She looked at me with red eyes. "Yes, Daughter."

"Princess has a confession to make."

"Daughter," Ollie said. "We *know*."

—

The letter from Sister Anne that arrived at our ranch house two years before had informed Ollie and Ray of my true identity. Ollie brought me the letter now. Sister Anne got right to the point. She was writing, she said, to impart certain information that had been withheld by the County Department of Welfare in 1962 and was now available to her via a source she was not at liberty to disclose, for legal reasons established by the Privacy Act of 1938 for Adoptive Charities chartered by the State of Iowa. Truly extraordinary circumstances had resulted in an unforeseeable coincidence. Sister Anne hoped to bring this new information to the attention of Ollie and Ray in the form of the revised and updated case history enclosed, before they learned it through other means, whether those means be the subject, Princess Hopkins, or others, be they friends, neighbors, family members, or general citizens known to her.

Whether the inauthenticity of the initial case history was a result of incompetence, error, or malice on the part of the county, Sister Anne did not know, but the absence of known fact when the subject became the responsibility of the diocese as represented by the St. Xavier's Convent required the history in question to be constructed on hearsay and guesswork. Technically, the deviation from fact was not sufficient cause to annul the legality of the transaction between the diocese and the Hopkins family. However, if Ollie and/or Ray should feel the error and/or omission threatened the foundations of the positive parental feelings harbored for the adoptee, thus affecting the strength of their long-term commitment, the diocese would not hold Ollie and Ray in breach of contract. It was a lot of big words for a simple admission on Sister Anne's part that she had lied and would take me back.

Page two was my revised case history. I was a female born March 9, 1950, in the Arnold Municipal Hospital. Weight, 6 lbs., 10 oz. Name, Crane Cavanaugh. Reared on Gravel Pit Road, substandard domicile subsequently condemned. No registered postal designation. Mother was one Letitia Grund. Mother's race, half German, half Sioux. Father unknown.

The letter was dated January 17, 1965. "Why didn't you say anything until now?" I asked Ollie.

"I seen a counselor!" Ollie said. "Itty-bitty, funny-lookin' fellow with glasses and a high voice. Cost me twenty-five dollars! Ray threw a fit. Fella said to be patient or I'd spoil your emotional development. Said to sit tight. Said you'd bring it up when you were ready."

Ollie and I looked at each other for a moment as if we'd just met. This woman really loved me. Too bad there was more bad news. It would just have to wait. I took down my hair, removing each bobby pin carefully so I wouldn't chip my nice manicure, allowing the curled locks to fall like ringlets all around my head.

Ollie's red eyes softened a little, taking pleasure in the sight of me. "Princess?"

"Yes, Ollie."

"We never tried your hair curled like that before."

—

"At least you're valedictorian," Ollie said to me in the morning. I threw up.

Delay was not a tactic you found in microbes. You found it in man. Man delayed when his emotions were ahead of him, behind him, or beyond him. Which was so often, it made for a lifetime of hesitation, procrastination, and avoidance, all popular forms of delay. To act, to speak up, to take charge of the present sometimes felt impossible to man. Instead, man trudged guiltily along in his rut, unable to speak up, waiting for the bomb to be dropped by heaven, fate, or the local busybody.

I was starting to show. Each morning, my head hung, my feet dragged as I entered the kitchen. I promised myself as Ollie and I sat down at the dinette table to eat our cornflakes that I would blurt it out. But each morning, my voice stuck in my throat. I left the revelation up to Ollie. "Gadzooks, Princess!" she finally said one morning. My high potbelly was sticking straight out. "Grace Paludy was right! You're pregnant!" I told her I was indeed. I named Jump.

—

I missed my own commencement. My triumphant valedictory speech went unspoken. The principal himself, I was told, when citing my numerous honors and awards, stumbled over my first name almost every time, "P-P-Princess," arousing titters.

It wasn't the fit of the commencement gown that kept me home on graduation day. That pleated tent would have easily disguised my delicate condition. It was the shame. Would they hiss in front of poor Ollie? Would they boo? Would they egg me? Would the Wickets be there?

Ollie and I walked up the shore road and knocked on their front door. It took awhile for Mrs. Wicket to let us in. She was wearing a bathrobe. The skin around her right temple was the off-yellow color of a bruise a week away from being healed. She led us into the living room and invited us to sit on plaid furniture that was ripped at the seams. Her large, murky, unshaven boyfriend sat in the kitchen in a dirty T-shirt with his back to us. Every bone in his body was mean.

Ollie spelled it out. Daughter was in a fix. Daughter wasn't going to St. Vincent's Home for Unwed Mothers in Dubuque like the Paludys made Donna Stark do. No, the Wickets were going to deal honorably with a little gal who'd won the Westinghouse National High School Science Award and was valedictorian of the senior class. Daughter was going to be wed. Jump was going to bring honor, not shame, to the Hopkins family—and bring it soon—by making things right, preferably before the end of June.

"Jump?" Mrs. Wicket called to her son. He came out of his room, hollow and useless, except for being male. He had tried to climb out his bedroom window when he saw us walking through the knee-high grass to the door, but his mother's boyfriend manhandled him back into the house. "Is this true?" Mrs. Wicket said.

Jump looked at her boyfriend's menacing back, not at us, to answer, "Yes."

Ollie whipped out the spiral notepad she had ready in her purse. She flicked the point of her ballpoint pen into action. She made the arrangements in her halting, downhill handwriting. We got up to leave. "One more thing," Ollie said to Mrs. Wicket. "Don't wear lavender. I'm wearing lavender. You can pick any color dress in the rainbow but that. First dibs on dress color goes to mother of the bride." As long as there was the prospect of figuring out what to wear, Ollie was a stranger to despair.

—

"I ain't paying for no wedding," Ray said at night behind closed doors.

"It ain't a big wedding," Ollie said. "It's just us. And after that, she's Jump's responsibility."

"I ain't paying for no wedding for no two-bit whore," Ray said. "Her mother was a whore before her, and now she's a whore too. What's she going to do now—have another little whore?" Ray had a point.

"People make mistakes," Ollie said pointedly.

"Yeah," Ray said. "Well, they don't all turn out as good as me."

"I'll say," Ollie said. She did something romantic next. That was the key. Ollie always got her way. Daughter's photograph appeared in the local paper along with the discreet announcement of her imminent nuptials.

—

Ollie lifted my veil away from my face. There was a spot of something ashy on my cheek. Ollie licked her thumb and rubbed it, a little harder and longer than she needed to. Nothing other than everything was going to spoil Daughter's wedding day. But the spot wouldn't come off. Ollie's orchid wagged from side to side, along with her great rolling breasts, as she rubbed my cheek, rubbing and rubbing the spot of something she called "ashy." Except for that, we were ready.

Out in the sanctuary, seated in the pews, were our four guests. Ollie was still rubbing my cheek when Radley Stokes, the best man, came to get us. The ceremony was about to begin. He was ready to escort Ollie down the aisle. Ollie fluffed my veil back over my face and tried to straighten the gathers along the bodice. My dress was the Empire style favored by brides in the second trimester. We didn't have fun shopping for it at all.

Mrs. Paludy was at the organ. The minister gave her the signal. The processional started. I watched Ollie limp up the aisle on Radley's arm. Ray and I were waiting at the rear of the church. I heard the doors behind me open. There was an unceremonious altercation. The deacon was having words with someone who was trying to enter the church. My heart went yellow. I smelled our dust.

I ran to the church door and opened it in time to see a small, tentative woman traipsing down the front steps. The hem of her water-stained dress rose up in back and dipped down on both sides. Her black purse was cracked and mended with duct tape, its strap safety-pinned to the bag at both ends. She was unhealthily thin, with long skinny calves and dusty feet in broken shoes. "What was that all about?" Ray said to the deacon.

"Just some drunk," he said.

"Looking for a handout?" Ray said.

"I don't know what she was looking for," the deacon said.

—

Here came our cue—the music changed to the wedding march. Ray waved me urgently to his side, but I stayed at the open door. The thinness of the woman's back in her retreat moved me, the sight of her burdened, stiff little shoulders, the smell of her vodka. I watched her cross the street without looking. A car almost hit her. She took the blame, bowing and begging apologies to the driver of the car. At the bus stop she opened her broken purse and fished around for a token. The bus was coming. I looked at my sadistic, impoverished groom waiting for me at the altar. With a sudden wild unexpected love for myself, I left all the known disasters ahead of me behind and, instead of walking up the aisle with Ray to take Jump as my lawful wedded husband, I yanked my veil back over my head and ran down the church steps into the sunlight. I crossed the street and climbed up the black rubber steps of the bus before the hinged doors could fold shut on my train. I'd know the loving smell of that dirty, brown ponytail anywhere.

—

Reader, I hear you thinking: Is that any way to repay the kindness, patience, trust, loyalty, and love of the woman who'd been a true mother to me, the woman who'd taken all my weaknesses in stride, who strove to ensure my continuing welfare— to leave her standing there with her mouth hanging open at the front of the church where I was to be wed, a ceremony she'd still have to get Ray to pay for, while I jilted the groom, leaving behind a life of poverty and light torture to run away with my sister?

Listen carefully, all you wronged people who never did anything to deserve the slights and insults, the wounds and blows
inflicted on you by the people you loved who didn't or couldn't
or wouldn't love you back as much. I didn't want to hurt Ollie.
I didn't mean to hurt Ollie. I did what I did because my amygdala told me to.

—

My sister and brother had found each other. Next, they went
searching for me. But the Privacy Act, designed to protect the
reputations of nice families whose female members made mistakes, prevented disclosure of the identity of either the biologi-
cal parents or the legal parents of any adoptee. The law allowed
the county to correct state records, nothing more, sending the
accurate information via Sister Anne in one direction only, to
Ollie. My sister and brother were left in the dark.

—

That day in the waiting room at the county building, when
Jima climbed up on the seat of a chair to watch through the
door window as they led me away, she was put on a Greyhound
bus to Council Bluffs. She was seventeen, too old to be adopted.
They found a bed for her at the Home for Troubled Girls. The
girls there had broken and entered, they'd stabbed and shot.
Their self-esteem began with gratitude to any male who didn't
rape. They were too troubled. In their midst, Jima was offen-
sively innocent. Repeatedly, she got hurt. The director called
around to find her a safer place. She was not about to be a
mother, but she was unwed—that qualified her for the Home

for Unwed Mothers. They were happy to reserve her a bed. The director put her on a Greyhound bus to Dubuque.

The driver was tall and bald, with unambitious, affable eyes. He enjoyed handling the big steering wheel, keeping his elbows aloft, his arms crooked in Ls, chewing up a butterscotch Lifesaver every fifteen minutes to mark the passage of distance and time. Now and then he offered one to Jima, who sat opposite him so he could keep an eye on her. The bus stopped at the station in downtown Arnold to pick up passengers. The driver got out to drink a Coke and thumb through *Life*. Elizabeth Taylor was on the cover again. Her husband had just died in a plane and she'd already stolen Eddie Fisher from Debbie Reynolds.

From her seat by the window, Jima watched the comings and goings of the guests at the Sideman Hotel across the street. A familiar figure was standing stock-still next to the revolving door of the hotel. It was the awkward, unforgettable Swiss woman who'd come to the shack to sell her *The Children's Book of Knowledge*. Now she was dressed in the uniform of a hotel chambermaid, waiting for a ride home.

Before she could think twice, Jima shouldered her official Troubled Girls duffel bag filled with neatly folded new clothes. She climbed down the steps of the bus and crossed the street. Everything happened at once. The Swiss woman saw Jima coming with all of her earthly belongings. Her eyes grew round with excitement. Homesickness vanished from her face. Happiness gathered in a raw, foolish smile. The woman hadn't smiled since she left Switzerland. Her husband arrived in his white Rambler station wagon, queuing up behind a taxicab. Across the street, the bus driver noticed Jima's seat was empty.

He ran outside, looking urgently up and down the sidewalk for a brown ponytail. The Swiss woman climbed into the front seat of the Rambler. Jima climbed in behind. All she needed, she said, was a ride back to the shack. She knew these two would never take her there. She knew they would offer her a home.

—

Her name was Sybil Weidjczw—it wasn't spelled like Wide Jaw, just pronounced that way. We weren't orphans yet the day Sybil Weidjczw fell in love with us, Jima standing there in her dusty blue jeans with filthy me standing beside her, but Sybil was. Her parents had died in an avalanche while skiing in Italy. A Swiss couple in her Swiss village adopted her. She married an engineer from Lucerne, then he was invited to teach at Iowa State University right here in Arnold. They moved their quaint Swiss cuckoo clock and their well-designed, bright yellow, sturdy plastic kitchen utensils into a dark, homey bungalow built in 1910 two blocks from the campus. Sybil kept it spotless.

After she was fired from *The Children's Book of Knowledge* sales force, Sybil risked social stigma among the academics by joining the housekeeping department of the Sideman Hotel as a chambermaid. She loved making beds with stiff, clean, starchy sheets, scouring sinks with bleach, sweeping linty carpets clean, stealing silverware, one piece at a time, from the messy room-service trays. She taught Jima how to clean. Jima hired on too.

They whisked through rooms in record time, side by side, from eight in the morning until four in the afternoon. For Jima, Sybil saved liquor. Wine still in the bottle. Whisky still in the glass. If pickings on those fronts were slim, Jima unscrewed the caps of the miniature Smirnoffs, drank the little bottles dry, and chalked it up to a guest. In return, Jima helped Sybil pilfer silverware. Sybil was going for a full place setting for twelve, including serving pieces.

"There's a hole in me where my folks disappeared," Sybil told Jima one day as they sat in the bridal suite, looking out the window. Beyond the bus station, the river was brown. The newlyweds had checked out. "That's why I steal."

Sybil's observation gave Jima insight. "There's a hole in me too, where my sister disappeared," she said.

"That's why you drink," Sybil said. There was more to it than that, but Jima let it slide.

Sybil lifted the heavy silver domes covering the room-service entrées. The newlyweds had left behind an untouched pair of Sideman Club sandwiches—three slices of white toast, each thinly spread with mayonnaise and stacked with layers of chicken breast, lettuce, and bacon. The whole thing was then sliced like an X from corner to corner. Each triangular quarter was gored with a frilly toothpick to keep the layers level. It was a BLT built for a queen, though it could not be tidily eaten in public.

Jima watched Sybil to see how it was done. First she removed a toothpick from a triangular section and laid it neatly on the edge of the plate. Then she picked up the triangle with both hands, holding it between thumbs and index fingers, while gracefully arching all other fingers in the air as if this were ballet. Before chewing, she put the section down carefully, like putting a sleeping baby to bed. She chewed with her lips completely closed, patting them lightly with the linen napkin before lifting up the section for the next tidy bite. Jima prac-

ticed until she got it right. This carefulness, this ceremony, this
pause between bites showed respect for the structure of a sandwich as great as this.

—

At home, Sybil and Jima cooked Swiss food for Ez, grinding
veal for homemade weisswurst, stewing tripe with borlotti
beans for soup. For the most part, Jima was horrified, both at
the process and the result, but Ez was charmed to savor the
aromatic steam of true Swiss specialties rising from a soup pot
here in central Iowa.

After dinner, Jima learned to sew. She was too grateful and
too polite to guide Sybil toward the dresses, skirts, and jacket
patterns that suited her. Instead, to reward Sybil for loving her,
she embraced Sybil's terrible, limited taste, four-gore skirts
and collarless jackets in tedious prints and dull pastels. As they
sewed, Sybil recounted tales of the people she grew up with
in her village in the Alps. She told these tales intimately and
casually, as if Jima knew the families and the farms, the towns
and shopkeepers, the mules and goats as well as she did.

There was the shortsightedness of the Schmidt brothers,
two goatherds who cheated an honorable veterinarian out
of nine hundred francs for a Caesarian section on their prize
milk goat, then, two years later, watched the whole herd die of
pneumonia when the vet got revenge by refusing to drive up
the mountain to their farm with antibiotics.

There was the sadness of Anne-Marie, the young bride left
standing at the altar waiting for her groom while his brother
got him drunk, so drunk he fell out of his cart on the way to his
nuptials and was crushed under the wheels.

There was the nastiness of Irene, the stepmother who blatantly favored her own three daughters by the vicar over his first-born son, whose mother had died in childbirth. Unbeknownst to the vicar, she beat that little lad with so many blows to the head that he became an idiot. When the woman's daughters were grown, they hated the woman and would have nothing to do with her. Only the little idiot stood by her, knowing nothing of her cruelty, remaining slavishly devoted, caring for her in her helpless old age.

So thickly did Sybil apply this lore that when Jima stood before the full-length mirror, dressed in a finished garment of Sybil's design, she felt like a ghost from Sybil's village, materializing here and now in the upstairs hall to memorialize the harsh hand of fate on the Alpine mountain of her birth.

—

When Jima first set eyes on her husband-to-be, he was naked. She thought the bed he was sleeping in was empty—he was that thin. She whipped off the top sheet, waking him from an apparently exciting dream. They were both impressed. His name was Omen Vertz. He was a thirty-year-old Latvian itinerant custom automobile upholsterer with a library degree. He was balding at the temples, with dark, cultured eyes, elegant philosophical cheekbones, and a pointed, elitist chin. His skin was the color of sand. He wanted to see her again.

Sybil stole a dress from the hotel laundry, royal blue taffeta with a scoop-neck, a dropped waist, and a stylish sweep of skirt cut on the bias. Sybil had admired it in the hotel room of the optometrist's wife. Their big party was over. The wife wouldn't miss the dress if it took an extra day to recover from housekeeping. Omen was waiting for Jima at his table at Festa Italiana, the narrow little restaurant festively painted red, white, and green where he liked to dine when he was in town. The owner, Queenie Martini, a dewy-skinned, practical woman, sat at the bar, thumbing through a jewelry catalog while her three sons took turns waiting on tables, bussing, and cooking. Omen liked to sit there for hours, smoking, drinking, and brooding by candlelight, his eyes cast back with sophisticated regret to his glory days as a playboy in Riga.

Walking up to the implausibly cheerful façade, Jima caught sight of her reflection in the window glass. Stabs of guilt upset her equilibrium. The stylist at the Sideman salon had blow-dried her hair straight down like a folk singer's. Jima looked beautiful. She wasn't supposed to be beautiful. That was for other females, confident ones who drove men mad. But judging from the enamored expression in Omen's eyes as he looked through the window at her just now, tonight she was exactly that. He leapt to the door to open it for her. From the bar stool, Queenie turned her head Jima's way, smiling the intimate smile of welcome she clairvoyantly reserved for strangers she would come to know well.

They were married by a justice of the peace who was also president of the Arnold Classic Car Club. They exchanged vows while riding in Omen's cream-colored 1936 Stutz Bearcat with red leather interior. A caravan of classic cars followed in their wake, along the old tree-lined highway to the Arnold Country Club for a feast of Iowa beef. Photographs of the event still hang on the Car Club walls today, where members referred to it often as the best big bash there was. Omen went off to Omaha in the Stutz to upholster a 1956 Bentley Continental

Saloon for a wheat tycoon, and Jima moved into the one-bed-room apartment over Festa Italiana that had just become their marital abode.

We were there now. I was standing in my wedding dress, looking at a photograph of Jima in hers. We had waded through assorted items amassed on the floor—toys, vases, puzzles, books, figurines—to get close enough to the wall to see the framed wedding portrait. In the portrait, her ponytail looked clean and shiny. All of her hair made it into the clasp. She was proud of the dress. "Sybil made it," she said. With its long, gored, cuffless sleeves, its low, beautifully square neckline, its slim, straight skirt, ever so slightly wider at the hem than the waist, the design was a miracle of modern fashion understate-ment. Sybil had borrowed a dress to copy from an unknowing hotel guest from Paris, France. "It came from a store spelled D-I-O-R," Jima said to me. "Ever heard of it?"

"Oh, yes!" I said. At Diamond's, gowns by Dior were seen by appointment only on the highest floor.

"That's Jeremy," she said. Thumbtacked to the wall was a wallet-sized photo of a wounded five-year-old. His eyes were dark, sophisticated, and insecure. His two buckteeth rested soberly on his lower lip. His hair grew raggedly down past his ears. His slender little shoulders barely filled out the Underdog sweatshirt. The smile he forced for the school photographer was sweet, apologetic, and sidelong like his mother's. "Couldn't ask for a better kid."

"Where is he now?" I said.

"Oh, he can't live *here*," Jima said. "I was declared unfit!" Her voice was cheerful. "Omen, he went home to Latvia to take care of his dying mother, or so he said. He never came back. They come and took Jeremy away from me one day when I was on the bus. They give him to Little Duck to raise. A farm is a better place for a boy."

She reached under the bed and pulled out a large, hard, blue suitcase. "You seen father on television, right?" she said. Her pale gray eyes brightened with pride. She punched the brass sprockets. "Well, here's Mother!" The suitcase popped open, exuding a dusty smell. I was face-to-face with Flat's disassembled bones. Me, Miss Science—I screamed. "Got these with a court order," Jima said. "Mr. Fanelli helped me. Found out the county was going to raze our place. Bein' as I lived there sixteen years, I had a right to the contents. They made me go at night with a deputy, though, so as not to cause problems."

We both looked at Flat. "I'll brush her off one of these days," Jima said. "Ain't she dainty?" She was, especially her skull. She seemed happier without flesh—no trace of fear, envy, sorrow, rage, regret. Jima snapped the lid shut. She was proud of the suitcase. We admired it longer than we had Flat. "Pretty neat, isn't it," Jima said. "This way I can take her grave with me if I ever move out west or something. It's Samsonite. Nearly new. Cost a dollar-fifty at the Salvation Army Thrift Center. A man donated it right afore I came in. He was movin' to Hawaii—get this—with nothin' more than a duffel bag. That lamp is his too." She pointed to a hideous orange thing with a cracked shade. You won't believe it, but almost everything in this place I got at the Thrift Center." I did believe it.

—

I needed water, but I couldn't get to it. The kitchen and bathroom floors were piled with industrial-sized containers of

Stanley Degreaser Concentrate, Degreaser Plus TM, Will-Do Mildew, Big Wally Wall Brushes, and Germ-X Disinfectant Spray. Eighteen years had gone by, and my mother was still between me and the things I needed. Jima explained. Tit was now an official sales representative for Stanley Home Products. She earned extra points for every multigallon order. She called Jima monthly to fill her quota. Tit was living in Tama with a full-blooded Indian named Mitch. To supplement the Stanley income, they traveled the width and breadth of Iowa, teaching the elderly to tango. "Ta-da," Jima said, handing me their how-to book, locally printed in full color with twenty-four step-by-step, easy-to-follow lessons. There she was on the cover, my mother, with a man's thigh between her legs. He was a young, good-looking, vacant Indian, six feet tall and cylindrical in shape, wearing a beaded headband and a tux. His skin was amber, his hair long, straight, and black. Tit was not only straddling his thigh, she was doing a back bend with her arm high over her head, her brown hair falling in waves to the floor, her armpit suggestively bared. Even with her face upside down, she was beautiful.

—

From Queenie we borrowed maternity clothes. Wearing a large, green, Gucci-print muumuu, I walked to the bus stop with Jima. We took the number nine to the end of the line. We ambled up the lane to the hog farm. A slender, stationary five-year-old silhouette, playing sentry at the water pump in the front yard of an old, white, two-story farmhouse, was galvanized into motion at the sight of Jima coming around the bend. Jeremy hurtled himself toward us sidelong, chin first, with open arms and slightly closed eyes. Loping along in the wake of his nephew, still stately, still severe, still Jesus-beauti- ful with his Sioux cheekbones and red skin, was my brother, Little Duck. Our colony was recombined.

—

Little Duck had been working at the Masker Street garage the day the county took us away. He pumped gas and fixed engines for the Backauer brothers. Ronnie and Meyer Backauer were both barrel-chested men with long, thick arms, narrow hips, and short legs. They started their workday in clean, ironed uni- forms, shirts tucked in, pants belted. Within an hour, the shirt- tails were flapping free, the pant cuffs were dragging on the floor, abraded with garage grime. Their hairy bellies hung out over their belts as they reached up with a wrench to untwist a nut on a car on the lift.

Evenings, the three of them worked on Ralph Dilby's bright yellow 1940 Ford Coupe with the big black number 27 painted on the side. This week, they'd made it lighter, stripping it of glass and extra metal. They were planning to drive out to the dirt track, a 3/8-mile oval west of town, to watch Dilby test- drive the coupe in preparation for Knoxville on the weekend. The coupe was all that Little Duck cared about. The first time he heard it coming down Masker Street, Little Duck drifted spellbound toward the sound, squeegee in hand. He'd been cleaning a customer's windshield. The sound of the engine was a sound he'd never heard before, a sound of whispering excellence, of powerful, faultless internal combustion, primed to roar, but held in beautiful check. Dilby tooted the horn as he passed the garage that day. He turned the corner. Little

Duck moved after him, hypnotized and fulfilled, as if he could subsist on the exhaust from anything that mechanically sweet, quiet, and organized.

"You ain't seen Dilby race, son?" Ronnie said to Little Duck back in the garage.

"No sir," Little Duck said.

"Well." Ronnie smiled the slowest smile in the Midwest, the muscles of his cheeks just barely lifting the corners of his deadpan lips, his eyes brightening two degrees as he recalled a beautiful turn in a recent race. "You will."

Little Duck joined them Friday nights as they towed Dilby's coupe to Knoxville. The Knoxville track drew drivers and fans from hundreds of miles around. They raced all weekend—hot rods, dragsters, and stock cars. A new fence circled the track. The track was graded to create banking in the turns. Lights were installed so they could race at night. Little Duck joined the Backauers in Dilby's pit. Nine times out of ten, when the checkered flag waved, it was the yellow coupe with the black 27 that was first across the finish line.

—

But that day, Little Duck had felt dislocated. There was a keening deep inside, a high-frequency discord. He dropped a wrench. Or it dropped him. He lost a piston ring. Or it lost him. He was struggling, and he didn't know why. His limbs felt heavy, his mood mournful. After work, he begged off driving to the track with the Backauers. Instead, he walked home along the railroad tracks. *Bam-bim, bam-bim, bam-bim.* He heard the county's hammer at the top of the ridge. Coming down the flats, he saw two men nailing plywood over the windows of the empty shack. He was nineteen, too old to be a ward of the state, but he hid anyway, sliding down the railroad bank, crouching under the transom. He waited until he heard them leave. They cranked up the engine of their truck. Their tires lunged over the railroad tracks. Silence. He climbed the bank and walked home.

Signs he couldn't read were nailed to the boarded-up windows. Two-by-fours were pounded in an X across the door. The shack was roped off on all four sides. His sisters were gone. He felt unstable. The way the boughs of the maple tree were scraping against each other in the wind had the eerie pitch and cadence of human speech. It sounded like Revelation: *And there appeared a great wonder in Heaven; a woman clothed with the sun, and the moon under her feet and upon her head a crown of twelve stars. And she being with child cried, travailing in birth and pained to be delivered.* It was Revelation. It was Flat. She'd let them board up the shack with her still in it. *And there appeared another wonder in heaven.*

He pounded on the boards covering the window. "Flat." Her voice stopped. There were still tools in the pharmacist's garage. With a screwdriver and a claw hammer, he pried away the two-by-fours and slipped through the opening of the front door. In the half-light of dusk, he saw the wild whites of Flat's eyes as she cringed under the cot, her head turned toward Little Duck with an embarrassed expression, as if she'd been caught red-handed in a display of genuine heartfelt emotion by a malevolent stranger. "Come on," he said. "You can't stay here." She turned her face away. He reached for her hand. She took it back, curling her fingers into a closed fist as if she didn't plan to use her hand anymore. "God damn you, you can't stay here," he said. She folded herself away from him to reflect fury at the sound of his blasphemy. "I'm sorry, Flat," he said. "I'm sorry for taking the Lord's name in vain." She wouldn't move or speak.

He slipped back out through the gap he'd pried at the door. He lingered there. Night fell. The autumn moon floated out from behind a cloud and hung in the sky. He couldn't leave. The cloud thinned out. The air cooled as it rolled across the lake. The moon rose higher, free of the clouds. What was he waiting for? He didn't know until he heard it. *And behold a great red dragon having seven heads and ten horns and seven crowns upon his heads.* That was it. Now that she was picking up where she left off, he could leave her. He walked back into town.

———

Meyer got his spare room ready. Little Duck moved in. The three men worked all week together in the cool darkness of the garage. Ronnie and Meyer loved to hear about Little Duck's problems with women. Weekends, they headed for Knoxville, checking into the Starlight Motel. One Saturday night, Little Duck was lying on his back in the pit halfway under the coupe, tinkering, when Ron came to get him. "Some girl wants to come in here and see you," Ron said. Girls were always wanting to come in here and see Little Duck. This one was different. "Says she's your sister."

Ron would remember the pause. The stillness of the tool in Little Duck's grasp, the way his head remained stationary in the uncomfortably upraised angle that put a crick in a man's neck. It was a pause not of hesitation. It was a pause of completion, the completion of a natural cycle. Ron would remember the grace of the kid, noteworthy under the circumstances, the reliance on method that prompted him to rise to his feet at the same speed he always rose, to place the wrench in its slot in the tool kit with the same calm he always did, and to walk forward in his easy lope to the gate of the pit as if this happened every day. Except the look in the eyes was new. Ron had never seen this look before. It was layered with boyhood things, affection, adventure, companionship, tenderness. There was a small protective smile in one corner of the kid's lips. Ron had never seen Little Duck smile.

The skinny, dusty little thing at the gate couldn't weigh more than ninety pounds. She emitted a high-pitched squeal, jumping up and down like a five-year-old when she saw her brother. Little Duck picked her up in his arms like a bride and twirled her around in circles.

—

The thing that impressed Little Duck the most about his sister was not the foreign classic car upholstery guy who came to Knoxville all the time. It wasn't the skinny, smart-looking year-old baby or the two blobby, humorless, Swiss stepparents. It was that institutional life had taught her to read. He called up Literacy Volunteers. They assigned him to a twenty-year-old student at the Teachers College with brown eyes and a cute pixie haircut. Her name was Diane.

"*Di-ane!*" Little Duck said. "I just got rid of a *Diane*." It was true. He had somehow gotten mixed up with a cloyingly maternal female racing fan, a rich woman with a vague figure—breasts like small tumors, no waist—who ground her teeth at night and during the day sunk them into him. Some women were easy to leave. This one was near impossible. Ronnie and Meyer had been hiding him in the metal locker when she came in to get gas and asked for him.

Little Duck sat face-to-face with his second Diane twice a week for an hour for a year. The sight of him, so masculine and self-assured, yet unable to do what most people could do, pursing his lips to pronounce with effort a simple, obvious word like *house*—it was erotic to Diane. Her brown eyes got to him. He stuttered in front of them for a year as they caressed him with infatuated encouragement. When he graduated, he couldn't say good-bye. Stuttering all over again, he asked her to marry him.

"You what?" Ronnie said.

Somehow, in the space of two years, Little Duck ended up with a house and two kids. It was nothing he wanted. He wanted to be at the racetrack. He maintained the racing-oriented schedule he'd had as a single man. He was almost never at home. One weekday night, he walked into his bedroom at 2:00 a.m. with one sock missing. The light was still on. His second Diane was sitting up waiting for him, wanting to know where he'd just been. He admitted it. He'd been to see Dolly.

"*Who?*" Ronnie said.

Little Duck explained. Dolly was the fun, destitute woman who lived in the blue trailer, who the boys and men of Arnold paid to have sex with. Dolly had a passion for Hostess Cup Cakes. Little Duck had been bringing her a pristine pair still in the package since he was twelve. "She's got all kinds of tricks," Little Duck told Ronnie, "to make you enjoy things, prolong things, you know, relax you. She's got some pretty clever pressure points here and there, I tell you," Little Duck said. "Dolly and me go way back."

"I hope you didn't tell your wife all this," Ronnie said.

Little Duck offered a sheepish affirmative, lowering his forehead, raising his eyebrows, his lips in a light frown.

"Meyer," Ron said, "get the spare room ready. Duck here's about to be single."

———

Little Duck met his third Diane when he dinged her truck. He was twenty-four. Divorced a year. Never saw his daughters. Never paid his wife. He was pulling into a parking space at the Arnold diner. He was laughing at something on the radio. He closed his eyes for a fraction of a second and put a scratch on a new Ford truck. It was red. Cantankerous people bought new red trucks. His third Diane saw it all, sitting inside at a window table. Her eggs over hash had just arrived. She stomped out the door and met Little Duck chin-to-chin as he got out of his car. "You call that driving?" she bellowed. She was stocky. Her short, kinky, dyed red hair showed obvious black roots. Her blue eye shadow had been applied in the distant past. It should have been either removed or refreshed. She was forty if she was a day.

"That scratch was there before I got here," he yelled back.

"That's a bald-faced lie," she said. "You weren't looking. Your eyes were closed. You were laughing. You scratched my new truck," she said, jabbing her index finger in his chest. She was strong. "You're going to admit it. And you're going to fix it."

He did both. He liked the way she jabbed him. As a peace offering, he brought it back to her detailed with flames whispering away from the rear wheels.

—

His third Diane had her own house on her own hog farm. The second Diane had the house Little Duck gave her. She had a new man friend living there now, which irked Little Duck until he realized he himself was living in the house his third Diane's husband had given *her*. Then all things seemed equal. Indirect, but equal, though somewhere in the future, there was a man with no house—the last man to get divorced. Which seemed to imply that somewhere in the past there was a woman with two houses. He was sure of the inequity, though he couldn't prove it.

This Diane was a hardworking, teetotalling breeder of purebred hogs. Her Hampshire boars were famous in breeding circles. Big Kahuna, the product of Sweet Look and Blockbuster, won $98,000 one year. For every dose of his semen she sold, Diane got $250. Her farm was a great, stinky, muddy, well-run thing west of town. Every week, middlemen flew in from England, South Africa, Poland, and France, coming to the farm to load up on boar semen to hand-deliver to the hog breeders of the world. Diane's year was packed with hog-related events, the World Class Bred Gilt Sale in Oklahoma, the National Barrow Show in Minnesota, the Weanling Extravaganza, conferences in Texas and Kentucky, the World Pork Expo right here in Iowa down in Des Moines. She had her own smoker; she sold her own brand of sausage, bacon, and ham.

Her farmhouse was a creaky, sprawling, messy thing two hundred years old. She stored her hog business paperwork on the dining room table. Her hog citations were hung on the living room walls. Figurines and knickknacks that glorified country life were distributed throughout the house where they made no sense. A generator was stored in the entrance foyer. The mudroom in back was rife with snow shovels, garden spades, hoses, and brooms. It was the home of a person who was always dirty, always outside.

Now, Jeremy lived with them. When Diane's people came to the farm from outlying towns for summer holidays, they became Jeremy's family too. They filled up two picnic tables under the pines. Red-checked oilcloths covered the tables. Diane's sisters and aunts unpacked hampers of fried chicken, homemade pickles, peach, cherry, and apple pies. Little Duck sat there, one of them, with Jeremy by his side, pleased and amazed at the naturalness of the plenty, the quiet affection, the peaceful enjoyment of one another's company. These things had been important to him all along. He was grateful for them now, and would never be able to take them for granted.

At dusk when the food was put away, the men gathered in the side yard to play horseshoes. The younger ones threw the Frisbee. The dogs played Frisbee too. Later, the poker chips came out and the cards got dealt. Sometimes when the game went late, Little Duck glanced in awe at his third Diane, fanning out her hand, hunkering down in her seat, wearing her glasses not over her eyes, but on top of her head. The faint scent of hog shit lingered on the heels of her boots. *How'd I get here?* he asked himself. He never closed his eyes when he drove. Closing your eyes meant losing control.

And later yet, when they'd all gone home and Jeremy was asleep, and the sky crackled with distant warning thunder, he and his third Diane lay in bed, eyes open, waiting for the storm.

The deluge came. They listened for a while, then closed their eyes. The sound of rain produced the best, most peaceful sleep they got all year. In the morning when the sun came out, the humidity made the corn plants sweat and steam. The leaves thickened and lengthened, growing greener than green. Little Duck listened. Was that soft crackle the sound of corn growing? Little Duck's breath caught in his throat then. Those fields he'd gazed at for hours on end when he was young, standing at the fence, watching the farmer farm, fields that stretched all the way to the horizon on either side of the railroad tracks—this was one of them.

—

Jima drank herself into a stupor on the porch. Little Duck gave me the tour of the hog farm. Jeremy tagged along with us. We stood in the cool shade of the pole barn, looking at the cream-colored vintage body of the 1936 Stutz Bearcat with its polished spoke wheels and red leather interior. It was creased, smashed, and crumpled in a crescent where Jima had wrapped it around a tree. She'd already told me the story, proud of the fact that she was so drunk, she'd gotten away without a scratch. "You'd best find another situation," Little Duck said to me now. He looked down at Jeremy. "You won't do well there anymore than he did."

Jeremy looked into my eyes to testify. As further proof, he took ahold of his uncle's hand. "You're always welcome at the farm," Little Duck said. I thanked him, but psychic fusion from the past had simplified that choice for me. That twenty-three-year-old woman with the pale gray eyes, gray skin, and teeth the color of weak tea, who drank a minimum of a quart of vodka a day—and who had once been my sister who'd raised me and saved me, who carried me everywhere, watching, watching—I could never leave her side unless my amygdala told me to.

—

That said, reunion was overrated. It was an unsettling, invasive, disorienting, inexpressible hallucination—and unlike other hallucinations, it never seemed to end. Jima's last act of the night was to let in the dogs. Those three, mangy, wild-eyed, untrained, attention-starved mutts confined behind the restaurant in a chain-link-fenced pen the size of a Volkswagen bug were dogs Jima had "rescued" from the animal shelter. They were flea-ridden, hungry, and hoarse from barking all day. She made it up to them at night. We five shared a bed.

I lay there staring at the ceiling with wide, terrified eyes, gulping oxygen out of the stale, itchy, humid, dog-hair-packed air. One of the dogs always dreamed he was running. No matter which way I tried to turn, his strong forelegs and sharp paws found and kicked my poor pregnant stomach. It was difficult to admit I was hungry here. To feed myself, I would sneak into the alley behind the restaurant kitchen and go through Festa Italiana garbage, looking for meatballs. The three dogs barked themselves hoarse with envy.

One hot afternoon, Queenie's son, Tony, caught me in the act. He led me into the kitchen, sat me down, and fed me. After that, he saved the special of the day for me to sample. All I had to do was knock on the alley door, and he'd let me in. And that's where I was one stifling August noon, in the kitchen with Tony, when I passed out. I hadn't felt right all day. The baby hadn't moved for a week. Now, suddenly, it wanted out two months early. The telltale series of hard-slamming, wrenching, searing internal blows known as labor pains were so violent, I fainted. Tony rushed me to Arnold Community Hospital.

—

I came to to the sound of television—*The Price Is Right*. Jima was sitting beside my bed in an orange plastic chair, reeking of vodka, picking up tips from Bob Barker to aid her Thrift Center discoveries. The walls in Maternity were supposed to be pink. These were white.

"Was it a girl?" I asked Jima. She said it was. "Where is she?" I asked. Jima said she was born still. I looked at the ceiling for a sweet, oval, female face. Nothing yet.

—

Thorazine was slowing down my brain to a heavy, worried churn, like a cement mixer turning for no reason other than to keep its load of wet cement from permanently hardening and wrecking the truck. It felt like my crotch had been sawed in half with a chain saw at great leisure, only to have everything in there hastily rearranged and stapled shut. I didn't need a tranquilizer. I needed a real painkiller, like my mother used to get from my father.

—

It was Sunday morning. I was about to be released. Jima was watching Big Duck on television, warming up the audience at Christ Town, preparing them for an announcement of untold new blessings to be made today by Dr. Jiggins. Jima watched him with her head cocked at the childish angle of unexamined adoration, until my brother walked in. Guiltily, she snapped off Big Duck. Little Duck hated Big Duck more than he should. Jima loved him more than she should. To me, he was still hollow.

With my brother on my right and my sister on my left, I hobbled down the hospital hall, through the lobby, and out the front door. Waiting at the curb was a surprise—Number 27, Ralph Dilby's bright yellow Ford Coupe. Little Duck helped me into the passenger seat and got behind the wheel. He was driving me home to the farm to live. As we pulled away from the curb, he tooted the horn at Jima, standing on the corner at the bus stop waiting for the number four. She waved good-bye. Sometimes you leave people behind, not because you have to, but because it's time to, not because they're torn from you, but because they're not.

—

Labor Day weekend, Diane's family gathered under the pines at the farm for one of their massive, delectable Iowa potlucks. Afterward, those of us who didn't play games sat on the front porch, rocking in rocking chairs, watching those who did. The shadows of the trees were long and strong in the late afternoon sun. The crickets were loud, filling the air with the sound of that plaintive end-of-summer chord. The air had a fallish bite to it. Up the lane to the hog farm came a teal blue 1957 Ford Thunderbird with Ted Fonic at the wheel.

I poured him a glass of iced tea. He sat on the porch, rocking with me. I'd received letters from ISU informing me of my room assignment, lab hours, and class schedule. But somehow, the information on Rush Week organized by ISU's sororities had been mailed to Ollie. Ollie was officially forbidden by Ray to have contact with me. She asked Ted Fonic to intervene, to come get the information and deliver it to me wherever I may be.

"Does she miss me?" I asked.

"I'll say," he said. "Her polio's coming back. She weighs half of what she used to weigh. She looks twice her age." He made it sound like an equation. "She cried when she showed me your room," he said.

"Was it still pink?" I asked. I was afraid Ollie had painted the whole thing gray and given it back to Ray.

"Oh, very pink," he said.

"Did she ask about—*it*?" I still couldn't say the word *baby*.

"Someone who works in the hospital told her," he said. "She hopes you're convalescing well." Ted Fonic smiled at me like ants probably smile when they're passing on a special directional signal leading to food. "Ollie and Ray have *gone back to church*," he said, vocally underlining my cue. "They're regular Methodists now. Ray especially. Ollie said Ray believes forgiveness isn't always deserved, but it is always possible. He won't miss a Sunday, always the nine o'clock service."

———

I borrowed heels, gloves, and a Sunday dress. And that's where I went, to the Methodist church at nine o'clock on Sunday morning. I walked down the aisle of the sanctuary and sat in the front pew. I opened the hymnal. I sang. *From sinking sand He lifted me, With tender hand He lifted me, From shades of night to plains of light, O praise his name, He lifted me.*

"Craaaane!" It was a bellow of the unapologetic hog-farmer variety. Ollie was waiting for me outside the church after the service. By her side was Ray. He looked different. At first I thought it was the suit and tie, but it was deeper than that. It was the way he let me look him right in the eye. There was redemption in his bright hazel irises, wisdom in the crow's feet fanning out toward the temples on either side. He invited me home for Sunday dinner.

Ollie *was* thinner. She did look older. She used a cane. I'd read up on it. Half the adults with childhood polio got it back. "I feel so weak," she said. "I get so tired. Some that get their polio back end up in a wheelchair."

"God will help us," Ray said, putting his arm around her.

I joined the church—me, the cutting-edge myrmecologist, whose rigorous, unflinching objectivity helped to identify the effect of kin recognition on foraging patterns of *C. pennsylvanicus*. I gazed up at the inexpensive stained-glass window of the Methodist church, and, with no twinge of conscience, I took Jesus as my Lord and Personal Savior. How? The answer was simple. I cheated. Faith, I knew firsthand, could not be trusted. Instead, my heart was filled with nostalgia. I let those two syllables, *Jeee-sus*, carry my nerves back to a time of enthralling, comforting equations of light in the purity of our shack, a place of blind, beautiful, yellow tranquility, dappled with the unsafe smell of my mother's red dress, the sweet, dirty smell of my sister's brown hair. How easy that made it. *Oh, what would I do without Jeee-sus, When the days with their shadows grow dim; When the doubt billows roll, sweeping over my soul, Then what would I do without Him?*

—

Ray moved me into the dorm. He waited in the car while Ollie and I browsed in the hippie store off campus. Ollie got a kick out of the fringed leather vests. She tried one on. Next she wanted a poet's shirt. She tired so quickly these days, we had to drag a chair into the fitting room so she could sit down. I ran back and forth to the racks for any new color or style that struck her fancy. Ollie's enjoyment of the world was undimmed by her reduced mobility. If anything, it was enhanced. Ollie had kept her Ollie-ness. It was something she didn't know she had, something unthreatened and Iowan, a way of being an ally that asked for nothing in return, an assumption of candor that fostered the same even in the wary. It was goodwill at the cellular level, with no punitive retractions should it turn out to be misplaced. Perhaps the whole world would be better off with more Ollie-ness. I knew I was. We both fell in love with the woven Guatemalan ponchos. Ollie got hers in turquoise. I got mine in rust.

—

And so it was, disfigured inside as well as out, sterile, ugly, and loved to the core, I charged up the steps of the exalted Hall of Science on the first day of college to study microbes. If Benjamin Franklin wore love beads and hip-huggers, he'd be a dead ringer for me.

Acknowledgement

The story of Crane Cavanaugh would not exist without the persistent enthusiasm of Denise Shannon, who sensed Crane's possibilities first in a three-page short story and fought for her at every length thereafter.

Permissions